CAUGHT SWIMMING BY MR. DARCY

PRIDE AND PREJUDICE VARIATION

☙

JANE ADELL

Copyright © 2023 by Jane Adell

All rights reserved.

No part of this book may be reproduced in any form or by any electronic or mechanical means, including information storage and retrieval systems, without written permission from the author, except for the use of brief quotations in a book review.

❦ Created with Vellum

CHAPTER 1

The sweltering sun bore down mercilessly on the verdant fields of Hertfordshire county as Fitzwilliam Darcy rode out on his favorite chestnut stallion. The heat was oppressive, leaving his finely-knotted cravat limp and his shirtsleeves damp with perspiration.

As he crested the gently sloping hill towards his favorite secluded pond, a delightful splash accompanied by a lilting giggle caught his rapt attention. There, upon the shore, lay a woman's clothes and delicate undergarments, and to his utter astonishment—in the pond's calm water—could it be? Elizabeth Bennet?

Mr. Darcy pulled up abruptly, his heart pounding like the drums of a military march. What on earth could she be doing here, frolicking in a state of undress?

He knew he should call out to her, announce his presence, and request her immediate withdrawal. Yet at that moment, he could scarcely remember his own name, let alone why her enchanting state of undress was considered improper. His throat seemed to close up entirely as he observed her splash and cavort in the crystalline pond, droplets of water glistening like diamonds on her exposed skin.

Never had he beheld a woman so unclothed outdoors, much less the woman he had secretly admired from afar these past months. The sight of Elizabeth's bare form awakened a feverish desire in him that made a mockery of his vaunted self-control.

He gripped the reins of his horse, torn between fleeing posthaste and lingering to watch her a moment longer—to sear every graceful line and curve into his memory. For so long had he yearned for a glimpse of her unguarded loveliness. Here she was now, a vision that surpassed even his wildest imagination, and he found himself powerless against the captivating allure of her beauty.

His ungentlemanly curiosity prevailed, and it was not until Elizabeth turned in the water that the spell was shattered—just in time for their eyes to meet, and for him to glimpse the dawning horror in her own. Her eyes widened and she released a startled shriek, submerging herself into the pond's depths.

Darcy's face flamed as if set ablaze. Never had he been so profoundly ashamed or so furious with himself and his own weakness. How dare he take such a liberty, ogling her without consent like some depraved voyeur? He spurred his stallion to hastily depart, but fate deemed it too late.

"Mr. Darcy!" she cried out, her voice laden with panic and mortification.

His cheeks burned as he kept his gaze steadfastly forward, even though every fiber of his being strained to glance back at her. "Please accept my sincerest apologies, Miss Elizabeth, for intruding upon your privacy. I shall be on my way immediately."

He heard the sounds of splashing and the rustle of clothing being hastily donned. The images these noises conjured threatened to unravel him entirely. His blood coursed hotly through his veins as he envisioned the curves of her dewy skin and the rivulets of water trickling down her chest.

At last, she called out, "You may turn around now, sir."

He complied with great difficulty, nearly groaning aloud at the sight of her. Though dressed, her raven hair cascaded loosely about her shoulders, tendrils of it clinging to the flushed skin of her neck. The memory of her half-clad figure assailed him anew, leaving him quivering with illicit longing.

Her face was the color of ripe cherries. "I am the one who must apologize," Elizabeth stammered, her own voice tremulous. "I did not expect anyone to encounter me here." She hesitated, gazing at him with parted lips as her bosom rose and fell rapidly. "I assure you I was simply...overheated. In this heat."

The words were whispered as if in a gossamer haze, threaded through with significance that transcended their apparent intent. Did she speak of the sultry warmth of the day, or of the almost palpable heat smoldering between them even now? Mr. Darcy's chest tightened, his breath catching as desire coiled within him like a serpent.

"Think nothing of it," he managed at last, his voice roughened with restraint. "Merely an accident and no harm done." He swallowed hard. "I shall keep this to myself and not besmirch your reputation in any manner."

"I appreciate your discretion," she murmured softly.

They regarded each other for a long moment, flushed with equal parts mortification and something more. Mr. Darcy clenched his hands into fists, every sinew taut and quivering with the effort not to close the distance between them.

He fought valiantly to master himself. How often had he dreamed of holding her, with no fabric to separate his skin from hers? At last, he managed a stiff bow, wrenching his gaze from hers. "Good day, Miss Elizabeth."

His voice was nigh unrecognizable, hoarse and thick with passion.

"Good day, Mr. Darcy," she replied, her tone echoing his own.

As he rode off at a breakneck gallop, he cursed himself for a fool as his mind swirled with the memory of Elizabeth rising from the water. He knew her image would haunt his every waking hour, a sweet torment he was not sure he wanted to escape.

～

Elizabeth hurried back to Longbourn, trembling with indignation and consternation. To think that of all people, Mr. Darcy should discover her swimming half-clothed! If she had awaited a punishment for her recklessness in seeking relief from the oppressive heat, this would be too cruel by far.

Venturing to swim in the secluded pond had been foolhardy, but the scorching heat had frazzled her senses. Now her impulsiveness had led to utter calamity. Even if the arrogant Mr. Darcy kept their encounter a secret, which she doubted he would, the memory of it threatened to torment Elizabeth for days to come. To have been so exposed before him was insufferable. She clenched her teeth as she hastened home, wishing she could purge the memory from her mind entirely.

She knew she should not have gone swimming in such an exposed location, but the stifling heat had been unbearable, and the pond's cool embrace too tempting. The memory of Mr. Darcy's gaze upon her, startled yet smoldering, was seared into her mind and refused to grant her peace.

Upon arriving home, Lydia greeted her sister with a teasing lilt in her voice and a knowing smirk that danced across her rosy cheeks. "My dear sister, did you not find the pond quite refreshing today? I daresay you were hoping a pair of fine eyes might happen upon you!"

Elizabeth's chest tightened, but then she breathed an inward sigh of relief as she realized Lydia was only jesting, as was her habit. She did not know the truth of what had transpired.

"Do not be ridiculous," Elizabeth retorted sharply, her eyes flashing. "I have no intention of tarnishing my reputation by cavorting half-clad for the benefit of strange men."

Lydia waved a dismissive hand, her curls bobbing with the motion. "Oh, come now, Lizzy, where is your sense of adventure? I am sure Mr. Wickham would not object to finding you in such a state!" She giggled again at the thought. "The look on his face would be quite diverting." Lydia laughed merrily. "My apologies. I could not resist. I know that you are far too proper to go swimming in the altogether!"

"Just so," Elizabeth said hastily, her heart pounding. "Now, I must lie down, for I have the beginnings of a headache."

"My apologies, dearest sister," Lydia said, though her smirk belied any real contrition. "I could not resist teasing you. I know you are determined to be dreadfully proper and serious at all times!"

With that, Lydia flounced out of the room, her silk gown rustling, already distracted by some new frivolous notion. Elizabeth breathed a sigh of relief at her departure, grateful that her sister's selfish nature had - for once - worked in her favor. Lydia's interest in the matter had been ephemeral at best, dissipating as quickly as it had formed.

For the remainder of the day, Elizabeth avoided her family, not wishing to endure any more of Lydia's idle teasing. But in the solitude of her room, her mind continued to torment her with unwanted visions of Mr. Darcy, his gaze both heated and tender as he caught her in his strong arms...

With a start, Elizabeth shook herself. It had been improper enough to be discovered swimming unclothed without conjuring ridiculous fantasies! Mr. Darcy was a gentleman and would never behave so lewdly. Allowing her imagination to run wild would only lead to further distress should she ever again face him.

As Elizabeth lay in her bed, sleep eluded her. Again and again, her thoughts drifted to Mr. Darcy, her mind creating a vision of him touching her at her waist as he lifted her onto his stallion. She told herself it was only her imagination, and yet her body tingled as if his hands were there heating her skin.

At last, she sat up with a groan and lit the candle at her bedside, determined to read a dull book of sermons until sleep overtook her. Anything to banish the tormenting vision of Fitzwilliam Darcy from her mind.

After hours of reading the dry, tedious text, Elizabeth's eyes, at last, grew heavy. She dared to hope that she had worn her imagination into submission and that it would trouble her no more with unwanted fancies. Blowing out the candle, she settled onto her pillow in the dark.

For a time, blessed silence reigned in her mind. But as she drifted towards sleep, new visions arose unbidden - of strong arms, soft lips, and a searing passion that dared not speak its name.

Despite herself, her traitorous thoughts had returned to Mr. Darcy. Yet these imaginings were not born of anger or distress but seemed only to stoke a slow, burning warmth deep within her. Amidst her vexation, she was startled to find a strange anticipation taking root.

∼

THE NEXT DAY was as sweltering as the first, the sun bearing down upon Longbourn without mercy. The heat was oppressive and irritable, putting all in poor temper—and yet Elizabeth dared not seek relief in her usual swimming spot. After the mortification of encountering Mr. Darcy, she could not risk being discovered again in such a state of undress.

When Lydia suggested they walk to the pond, Elizabeth hastily made an excuse about letters she must write. "Dearest sister, I have never known you to prefer writing letters over swimming on such a

CAUGHT SWIMMING BY MR. DARCY

scorching day! Are you certain you are quite well?" Lydia laughed.

"Perfectly well," Elizabeth said, hoping her cheeks did not betray her inner turmoil. "I have simply had a change of mood."

Lydia eyed her curiously but shrugged. "More's the pity. I shall be unbearably hot and bored without you today!" She flounced off, leaving Elizabeth equal parts relieved and guilty. She did not wish Lydia to suspect anything was amiss.

The following day was hotter still, and Elizabeth's agitation grew increasingly unbearable. Though longing for the cool relief of the pond, she knew it would be madness to venture there again. Not with the insufferable Mr. Darcy likely to appear without warning.

When the household settled in for their afte rest, the heat and anxiety within Elizabe reach a fever pitch. Despite her bett found herself stealing away to h Her heart pounding, she gla before removing her clo blessed coolness of t

As the water enveloped her, she released an immense sigh of relief. For a blissful half-hour, she swam at leisure, embracing the solitude and respite from the heat. Here, at least, in her secret place, she could find a measure of peace. She closed her eyes and let the worries, distress, and irritation of the past days melt away. But just as she moved to leave the water, she heard the snap of a branch in the woods. She froze in alarm, straining to see through the trees.

Her heart leaped with alarm at the thought it could be Mr. Darcy again, come to chance upon her in this state and subject her to further humiliation. But no —she banished the unwelcome notion at once. It was likely just a curious deer or fox emerging from the shade.

Despite his vow to keep their first mortifying encounter secret, she did not trust his honor. Every inch of her skin still tingled, though now from wariness rather than anticipation. She listened intently for any other sounds, but the woods had gone silent and still once more.

She took a deep breath, steeling her nerves. She had tarried here too long already in her state of undress. It was time to leave this place and return home before she was discovered in a scandalous position.

She began to dress in haste--but then froze at the sound of snapping branches and rustling leaves, drawing ever nearer. This was no forest creature making its way casually through the woods. This was the unmistakable sound of a man walking with purpose toward the pond, towards her.

Her heart flew to her throat as she glimpsed a familiar tall figure emerging from the trees. Mr. Darcy strode into view, scanning the pond and shore intently until it fell upon her.

They stared at one another for a long moment, motionless, the air between them crackling with unspoken tension.

CHAPTER 2

Beneath the relentless sun, Elizabeth's skin prickled with a warmth that had nothing to do with its rays. Acutely aware of her state of undress and the impropriety of the situation, she fought the urge to hastily finish dressing, realizing it would be futile by now. The damage was already done.

Her earlier shock at seeing Mr. Darcy manifested into seething annoyance. Had the man no sense of decorum? How dare he intrude upon her privacy so soon again, as if she held no value for it?

Defensively, she crossed her arms over her chest, clutching the edges of her dampened chemise while fixing him with a scowl.

Sensing the direction of her thoughts, Mr. Darcy frowned. "I did not expect to find you here again," he snapped, irritation etched into his finely sculpted features. "Do you mean to haunt this pond every waking hour, like some water nymph or sprite? How is a man to enjoy a leisurely walk without stumbling upon your bathing?"

Elizabeth bristled at his accusatory tone, tilting her chin up in a show of indignation. "I was not aware this pond belonged solely to your enjoyment, Mr. Darcy, else I never would have trespassed. If you wish to avoid such encounters in the future, may I suggest you announce your presence rather than skulking about like a spy?"

A flush crept across his cheek as her words struck true, though he made no immediate reply. At length, he said stiffly, "My apologies. I did not mean to offend."

"Of course not," she replied, her voice laced with sarcasm. "That has never appeared to be among your concerns."

Darcy's brow furrowed, scrutinizing her as if trying to discern her meaning. "I see you are determined to think ill of me, no matter my efforts at courtesy."

"Your attempts at courtesy leave something to be desired, sir."

"And yours often leaves something to be desired," he retorted sharply.

"I make no claim to courtesy where none exists," she said. "Yet I suppose that is the trouble—when we lack a proper sense of our own defects, it is difficult to perceive them in others."

"I lack a proper sense of my own defects?" The audacity of her words rendered him speechless for a moment. Then his lips curved into a sardonic smile. "It seems you see me clearly enough, Miss Elizabeth. For my part, I am aware of you, perhaps more than you realize."

His eyes smoldered as they traced the length of her, causing a flush to spread across her cheeks. She refused to give him the satisfaction of trying to cover herself. Let him look his fill if that was his purpose here.

"It seems I cannot escape you, no matter where my path leads," he grated.

But there was something raw in his gaze that spoke of deeper meaning. Elizabeth felt an answering tug in her chest, though she refused to examine it.

She lifted her chin defiantly. "You may escape me easily enough by respecting a lady's privacy. Now if you will excuse me, I have tarried here long enough."

Mr. Darcy's cheeks burned with humiliation. "My apologies. I shall walk to the other side of these trees while you dress, but I wish to speak with you—on a matter of importance."

Elizabeth frowned, waiting until Mr. Darcy's retreating back was entirely hidden before hastily donning her clothing.

From behind the trees, his voice carried over clearly. "Miss Elizabeth, given the unfortunate circumstances of our encounters, my honor demands that I take responsibility for compromising you in the eyes of the world."

She froze, one arm entangled in her sleeve. "Whatever can you mean, Mr. Darcy?"

"You know full well what I mean," he replied tersely. "Our meetings here have been highly improper and, if discovered, would irreparably damage your reputation. There is only one path forward that would satisfy my duty as a gentleman."

Elizabeth's heart leaped and sank at the same moment. She yanked her dress over her head and stomped to the copse of trees Mr. Darcy was hiding behind, unwilling to engage in this conversation in such a state of dishabille.

"Mr. Darcy," she warned.

He emerged from behind the trees, his features set with determination. "Do not argue, Miss Elizabeth. We must marry. Immediately."

"We must do no such thing!" Elizabeth cried. "Marrying against our wishes will help no one. I insist you not take responsibility for events beyond your control."

"The state of your reputation is well within my control," Mr. Darcy snapped, "and you cannot forbid me from doing the right thing. I will not be one of those cads who ruins a woman's good name and leaves her to face the consequences. It is entirely my fault you were discovered here, and I will not shirk my duty."

"Confound your duty and your honor too!" Elizabeth threw up her hands. "What of my wishes? Do they not signify at all, or must I enter into a loveless union to satisfy your misplaced sense of obligation?"

In a state of dishabille and righteous indignation, Elizabeth faced Mr. Darcy, their shared tension palpable. As the heated exchange continued, a flicker of vulnerability crossed Mr. Darcy's face, quickly replaced by an air of affronted pride.

"And this is your opinion of me?" he demanded, his voice low and strained. "You have said quite enough, Madam. I perfectly comprehend your feelings. Please forgive me for having taken up your time."

With a curt nod, Mr. Darcy turned on his heel, his tall frame retreating from Elizabeth with an air of wounded pride.

Elizabeth did not regret her harsh words to Mr. Darcy as she watched his figure disappear into the distance. While she had not meant to humiliate him, his arrogant and selfish behavior deserved censure. The idea of being forced into a marriage for the sake of duty and propriety was abhorrent to her, as was his purported mistreatment of dear Mr. Wickham.

She shook her head, wiping away the memory of his stricken expression after her retort. Let him think what he chose about her refusal—she owed him no apology or explanation. His pride would recover soon enough from the blow she had dealt in rejecting his suit. They came from very different worlds, and any attachment between them could only end in misery for her and ruination for him.

Still, much as she tried to dismiss the encounter from her mind, the image of Mr. Darcy in agitation kept returning to plague her. The heat in his gaze, the tension in his countenance, and the roughness in his voice as he entreated her, awakened an answering spark of awareness within her. Even as she hardened her heart against him, her body seemed bent on betraying her, kindling at the memory of his nearness with a visceral longing she dared not admit.

With a cry of vexation, Elizabeth hastened her steps back to Longbourn. She had dodged a bullet by refusing Mr. Darcy, but the danger was not entirely gone. Her heated response to his presence suggested she had not left her disdain unscathed. And Elizabeth feared that regardless of his character, she might never be free of her reaction to Fitzwilliam Darcy.

～

THE FOLLOWING DAY, the sun cast its warm golden rays upon the verdant lawns of Lucas Lodge, where laughter and lively conversations filled the air, heralding the prospect of a most delightful afternoon. The Bennet family, having received an invitation to partake in the lawn party, approached with eager anticipation. Elizabeth, her spirits soaring, engaged in animated conversation with her dear friend Charlotte Lucas. They discussed the latest gossip and marveled at the resplendent garden before them.

As they promenaded, Charlotte entertained Elizabeth with tales of a recent sojourn to Meryton. Elizabeth had just begun regaling Charlotte with the latest chronicle of her sisters' folly when she halted abruptly, the words expiring on her lips. Emerging from around the side of the house was the Netherfield party.

Elizabeth's breath caught in her chest, her heart pounding within her ribcage as her gaze darted among the arriving assembly. Noting her friend's distraction, Charlotte followed her gaze with a questioning look.

The Bingley sisters, adorned in the latest fashions, glided with practiced elegance. Louisa Hurst, arm-in-arm with her husband, conversed animatedly. The ever-charming Charles Bingley, his effulgent smile radiating warmth, appeared positively delighted to be in attendance.

And then, as though divining the focus of Elizabeth's attention, Caroline Bingley paused and turned back, unveiling the enigmatic Mr. Darcy striding last in the grouping. His tall frame and dark features were impossible to mistake.

A moment that seemed to stretch into eternity transpired as Mr. Darcy's eyes locked with hers, the air between them crackling with an intensity that belied the gaiety surrounding them. Elizabeth, her pulse quickening, wrenched herself from their connection, returning her concentration to Charlotte, who had been patiently awaiting her return to the conversation.

"Mr. Darcy is looking well," Charlotte observed, her tone neutral as she scrutinized her friend intently.

Elizabeth swallowed, endeavoring to regain her composure. "Yes, quite," she replied faintly, her voice betraying a hint of breathlessness.

As the afternoon progressed, Elizabeth tried in vain to divert her thoughts from Mr. Darcy. Laughter and music filled the air, while fragrant flowers and tempting delicacies teased her senses—yet nothing could compare to the captivating sight of Mr. Darcy's tall, commanding figure. The memory of encountering him beside the pond made her cheeks burn anew, and despite her efforts, her gaze was inexorably drawn to him.

Worse still was his expression when their eyes met across the crowded lawn: heat and barely restrained longing seemed to smolder in their depths as though he could see right through to the turmoil of desire and self-recrimination seething within her soul. How dare he look at her thus, as if they shared some intimate secret? As if he possessed rights over her that could only be granted by passion.

Despite her best efforts to maintain a light-hearted facade, Elizabeth's thoughts were consumed by the enigmatic gentleman, his heated appraisal of her dampened attire the day before, and his preposterous proposal of marriage the previous evening.

At one point, as Elizabeth found herself near the musicians, she glanced over to see Mr. Darcy engaged in polite conversation with a group of gentlemen. Their eyes met for a fleeting moment. She felt the familiar warmth suffuse her cheeks before she hastily looked away.

Charlotte, ever observant, had been watching the interactions between her friend and Mr. Darcy with growing curiosity. As she sidled up to Elizabeth, she could not help but remark, "It seems you, and Mr. Darcy have been quite preoccupied with one another this afternoon."

Elizabeth, caught off-guard by Charlotte's sudden inquiry, stammered, "I-I am not certain what you mean, Charlotte. Mr. Darcy and I have merely been attempting to navigate the social niceties of the event."

Her response, vague and tinged with nerves, only served to heighten Charlotte's suspicions.

A peal of raucous laughter from Lydia and Kitty pierced the air, drawing attention from several of the party guests. Relief washed over Elizabeth. "I must attend to my sisters," she said hurriedly, rushing off to curtail their boisterous behavior.

As she approached Lydia and Kitty, she found them regaling John Lucas with their animated retelling of a recent mishap in Meryton.

"Lydia, Kitty," she chided gently, "I understand that you are enjoying yourselves, but do try to remember that we are guests here and should comport ourselves with a measure of decorum."

"Very well, Lizzy. We shall endeavor to be on our best behavior." Lydia rolled her eyes playfully but nodded in acquiescence.

Satisfied, Elizabeth turned her attention to the rest of the party. She was pleased to see Mr. Bingley engaged in a quiet conversation with Jane, his admiration for her sister evident in his warm smile and attentive manner. Elizabeth's heart swelled with hope; she dearly wished for a match between Jane and the amiable Mr. Bingley, knowing it would bring her sister great happiness.

As the merriment continued, Elizabeth felt a sudden thirst and decided to fetch a glass of punch to quench it. As she approached the refreshment table, she found it momentarily unoccupied, save for the broad-shouldered figure of a gentleman whose back was turned to her. She moved closer, intent on retrieving a glass for herself, when the gentleman turned, revealing the unmistakable countenance of Mr. Darcy.

A momentary awkwardness settled between them, their eyes meeting with a sudden intensity that sent a shiver down Elizabeth's spine. Heat flooded her cheeks as the memory of Mr. Darcy's gaze upon her unclothed form rose unbidden to her mind.

Mr. Darcy cleared his throat, color visible at the tips of his ears. "Miss Elizabeth, may I...may I offer you some punch?" His usually composed tone wavered slightly.

"Yes, thank you," Elizabeth said hastily, grasping at the change of subject. She took the glass he offered, avoiding the brush of his fingers against hers, though the near contact still made her pulse leap.

They stood gazing at one another, a dozen words hovering on Elizabeth's lips, though she could not bring herself to utter a single one. The memory of Mr. Darcy's eyes, dark with longing as he gazed at her by the pond, threatened to rob her of speech entirely.

"You are most welcome, Miss Elizabeth." Mr. Darcy gave a curt nod, his cheeks nearly as crimson as Elizabeth's own. His dark eyes flickered to hers for a brief moment before sliding away, unable to maintain contact.

With their drinks in hand, Elizabeth and Mr. Darcy stood awkwardly for a moment, the silence between them growing heavier with each passing second. Elizabeth knew she must say something to break the tension, but her mind seemed utterly devoid of clever repartee.

CHAPTER 3

The muffled sound of approaching footsteps on the gravel path caused them both to start. Turning, they beheld Caroline Bingley approaching with an imperious air, her gown rustling softly as she moved.

"Mr. Darcy," she uttered with a false sweetness, drawing out each syllable like spun sugar, "I have been searching for you. Do you remember our delightful time at the Summer Exhibition in London? I have been longing to discuss our impressions of the remarkable artworks we had the pleasure of viewing. I was just describing them to Sir William Lucas, but your discerning taste and perceptive observations are so much more insightful than mine. I informed Sir William of that fact, and he is most interested to hear your thoughts on the pieces we admired."

Caroline's cunning attempt to draw Mr. Darcy away did not go unnoticed by Elizabeth, who found herself torn between annoyance and amusement. Despite her loathing for Caroline's manipulations, she could not help but be impressed by how seamlessly she had inserted herself into their conversation. The lady was nothing if not determined.

As Mr. Darcy reluctantly took his leave, he cast a brief, almost apologetic glance at Elizabeth. She met his gaze with a barely perceptible tilt of her head, acknowledging the situation for what it was: a transparent ploy orchestrated by a woman desperate to stake her claim on a man she believed to be hers.

Meanwhile, Caroline led Mr. Darcy towards Sir William Lucas, her step light and delicate as though she floated above the ground, the picture of grace and elegance. As they walked away, Elizabeth caught snippets of their conversation – Caroline gushing about the beauty of the art while Mr. Darcy offered restrained compliments in return, his tone polite but devoid of warmth.

Elizabeth watched them disappear into the crowd, feeling a mixture of curiosity and amusement. Though she had rejected Mr. Darcy's proposal, she couldn't deny that there was a certain thrill in watching him resist Caroline's advances.

Her spirits lifted even more when she spotted her dear sister Jane approaching with a radiant smile on her face. "You seem to be enjoying yourself today," Elizabeth observed, a knowing smile tugging at her lips.

A becoming blush rose on Jane's cheeks. "Mr. Bingley has been attentive," she confessed, her eyes sparkling with happiness. "We have had the most pleasant conversation, and he has asked if he might call on Longbourn again."

"Has he indeed?" Elizabeth exclaimed, clasping her sister's hands in excitement. "Jane, that is wonderful news!"

Jane's blush deepened, though her smile widened. "I do not wish to presume too much, but I find myself hoping..." She trailed off, a wistful note in her tone.

"That this may lead to an attachment?" Elizabeth supplied gently. At Jane's nod, she squeezed her sister's hands. "My dearest Jane, if any man is deserving of your affections, it is Mr. Bingley. I believe he is quite taken with you."

"Do you truly think so?" Jane asked a hint of wonder in her voice.

"I have eyes, have I not?" Elizabeth teased. "His admiration for you is as plain as the nose on my face. I shall be utterly shocked if he does not propose within the month."

"Lizzy!" Jane admonished, though her eyes shone with quiet joy. "You must not fill my head with such fancies. I do not wish to be disappointed if..." She flushed, lowering her gaze. "Forgive me. You are right that I should not borrow trouble where there is none."

"There, now." Elizabeth gave her sister's hands another squeeze. "All will be well. Of that, I am quite sure."

Jane's expression softened with gratitude. "Thank you, Lizzy. Your support and encouragement mean the world to me."

"As if I would not wish for your happiness above all else," Elizabeth said fondly. "Besides, it is selfish of me, really. If you and Mr. Bingley marry, I shall gain the most delightful brother."

Jane laughed, the sound light and musical. "You are incorrigible. Now, tell me. How have you been enjoying the festivities today?" Her gaze turned inquisitive.

Elizabeth grinned, mischief dancing in her eyes. "Why, I have had the most fascinating afternoon observing the determined campaign of a certain Miss Bingley as she attempts to ensnare our aloof Mr. Darcy."

Jane's expression turned to one of sympathy mixed with amusement. "Ah, yes. Her efforts have not gone unnoticed by anyone, it seems. Poor woman."

"I cannot help but admire her tenacity, though," Elizabeth replied with a laugh. "She is relentless in her pursuit and employs every weapon in her arsenal with remarkable skill. Alas, I fear her talents are wasted on a man who remains firmly resistant to her charms."

Elizabeth glanced across the lawn once more, only to find Mr. Darcy's eyes locked on her with an intensity that sent a shiver down her spine. It was as if he could not bring himself to look away, even as Miss Bingley continued her relentless pursuit.

As the afternoon wore on, the festivities drew to a close, and the guests slowly began to take their leave. The Bennet family made their way home, lively chatter filling the air as they recounted the day's events.

Upon arriving at Longbourn, the sisters gathered in the drawing room, eager to share their impressions and experiences of the party.

"Such a delightful gathering!" Mrs. Bennet exclaimed. "And I must say, Jane, you were looking positively radiant. It is no wonder Mr. Bingley could not keep his eyes off you."

Jane blushed demurely but said nothing. Elizabeth stifled a laugh, well aware of her mother's propensity for exaggeration and her ardent desire for a match between Jane and Mr. Bingley.

"And did you notice how attentive Mr. Darcy was toward our Lizzy?" chimed in Lydia, a mischievous glint in her eye. "I daresay he could hardly tear his gaze away from her."

Elizabeth rolled her eyes, though she couldn't deny the flutter in her heart at the mention of his attention. "Nonsense," she said lightly, trying to dismiss the subject. "Mr. Darcy was merely enduring the company of Miss Bingley, who seemed determined to monopolize his time."

Kitty snickered, clearly enjoying the gossip. "Perhaps," she ventured, "he was seeking solace in the sight of someone less...determined."

At this, even Elizabeth could not suppress a smile. She had to admit there was a certain satisfaction in knowing Mr. Darcy appeared immune to Miss Bingley's enthusiastic advances.

Mrs. Bennet, however, was not so easily deterred from her primary focus. "Never mind, Mr. Darcy," she huffed. "It is Mr. Bingley who holds the key to our Jane's happiness. I do hope he makes his intentions clear soon."

Her gaze settled on Jane, who blushed once more but remained silent. Elizabeth squeezed her sister's hand encouragingly, sharing a knowing look.

As the evening wore on and the conversation turned to other matters, Elizabeth found her thoughts increasingly occupied by the enigmatic Mr. Darcy.

His intense gaze seemed to have imprinted itself upon her mind, stirring emotions she could neither comprehend nor control. She couldn't help but wonder what lay behind those dark, brooding eyes – and whether she might ever truly understand the man who had so unexpectedly captured her attention.

∽

SEVERAL DAYS LATER, Elizabeth found herself strolling through Meryton with her sisters, attending to various errands for the household. The sun blazed radiantly overhead, casting a warm, golden glow upon the bustling town square that teemed with activity. Shopkeepers hawked their wares in exuberant voices as townspeople meandered about, exchanging pleasantries and gossip alike.

It was amidst this lively scene that Elizabeth happened upon Mr. Darcy, standing tall and commanding beside a splendid chestnut horse. He appeared to be awaiting someone or something, his dark eyes scanning the crowd with an air of impatience. As if sensing her gaze, he suddenly turned to look directly at her.

Elizabeth's breath caught in her throat, her pulse quickening as she met his intense stare. She offered him a polite curtsy, hoping to conceal her discomposure.

"Miss Elizabeth," he greeted her, inclining his head in acknowledgment. "A pleasure to see you again."

"And you, Mr. Darcy," she replied, her nerves causing her voice to quaver ever so slightly. Elizabeth stifled a smile. Before she could respond further, however, she felt a sudden tug on her arm as a young boy darted past, accidentally ensnaring her satchel in his haste.

In one fluid motion, Mr. Darcy extended an arm toward Elizabeth, the muscles of his broad shoulders taut beneath his impeccably tailored coat. Alas, his valiant attempt was thwarted by his chestnut steed's impatient snort and its head tossing, startled by the young boy.

Caught off balance, Elizabeth stumbled forward, her arms flailing in a desperate attempt to regain her footing.

To her mortification, she landed squarely in a puddle of water left by a recent rain shower, her dress now soaked and muddied.

Mr. Darcy's eyes widened in alarm as he tried to rush to her aid, yet could not leave his still-agitated horse unattended. "Miss Elizabeth, are you quite all right?"

Despite her embarrassment, Elizabeth couldn't help but laugh at the absurdity of her predicament. "Indeed, I am," she replied, attempting to rise with what little dignity she had left. "Though I seem to have made quite a spectacle of myself."

As Elizabeth endeavored to regain her composure, a group of dashing young officers approached, among them the ever-charming Mr. Wickham. "Miss Elizabeth," he said smoothly, extending a gloved hand towards her, "allow me to help you up."

His eyes gleamed with mischief as they met Mr. Darcy's, challenging him without uttering a single word.

Elizabeth accepted his assistance, acutely aware of Mr. Darcy's darkening expression. As she rose to her feet, the other officers gallantly flocked around her, proffering handkerchiefs and kind words to assuage her embarrassment.

Amidst the flurry of officers and the attentions they lavished upon her, Elizabeth caught sight of Jane and

Lydia emerging from a nearby shop. Their eyes widened in horror as they took in the spectacle before them.

"Elizabeth!" Jane cried out, hastening to her sister's side. "What has happened?"

Mr. Bingley, who exited the shop after them, appeared equally taken aback. His mouth fell open in shock, his cheerful countenance momentarily replaced with disbelief.

"I am quite well, I assure you," Elizabeth replied, attempting to wave off her sister's worry. "Merely a small mishap."

Lydia, unable to contain her laughter, exclaimed, "Oh, Lizzy! You do look like a drowned rat!"

Mr. Wickham stepped forward. "It appears the Bennet sisters are in need of an escort home. My fellow officers and I would be honored to accompany you all back to Longbourn."

The young men around him nodded enthusiastically, each vying to be the one to offer assistance.

"Thank you, Mr. Wickham," Elizabeth replied, her voice light and teasing, "I would be most grateful for your company."

Mr. Bingley chimed in, his natural amiability shining through once more. "Indeed, it is very kind of you and your friends, Wickham." His good nature stretched by the sight of a handsome officer offering Jane his arm.

The procession began with Mr. Wickham boldly offering his arm to Elizabeth, his eyes never leaving Mr. Darcy's. The tension between the two men crackled in the air like an impending storm. Elizabeth archly glanced back at Mr. Darcy before facing forward.

As they walked away, the jovial chatter and laughter of the officers and the Bennet sisters filled the air, contrasting sharply with the dark cloud that seemed to have settled over Mr. Darcy's countenance. He stood there, his handsome features marred by an unmistakable frown, watching the retreating group.

As the Bennet sisters and their dashing escorts commenced their journey back to Longbourn, the air around them buzzed with animated conversation and laughter. Lydia, the veritable embodiment of youthful exuberance, giggled and flirted without abandon.

Jane, the epitome of elegance and grace, listened with rapt attention to the officers' tales of daring and adventure. Her demure smiles and gentle encouragement served as a soothing balm to any bruised egos, eliciting further confessions and anecdotes from her captivated audience. The officers, in turn, were enchanted by her serene demeanor, vying for her attention like moths drawn to the flame of her radiant beauty.

Elizabeth, meanwhile, found herself engaged in an invigorating verbal duel with the ever-charming Mr. Wickham. Their rapid-fire repartee was akin to a masterful fencing match, each parry and thrust showcasing their keen intellects and shared appreciation for wit. Beneath the lighthearted banter, a palpable undercurrent of attraction hummed, adding a delightful frisson of excitement to their exchanges.

The procession continued merrily towards Longbourn, the sisters and their gallant companions enveloped in a whirlwind of laughter and blossoming affection. The atmosphere was charged with the exhilarating thrill of new connections and romantic possibilities, an intoxicating blend of emotions that left them all giddy with anticipation.

Unbeknownst to the merry group, a certain brooding gentleman, left behind in Meryton, wrestled with a tempest of emotions. The image of Elizabeth's sparkling eyes and laughter, paired with the simmering tension between her and Mr. Wickham, fanned the flames of both envy and desire.

As they approached the Bennet family's estate, Mrs. Philips happened to be passing by from visiting her sister. She took one look at the mud-soaked Elizabeth, surrounded by dashing officers, and gasped in delight. "Oh, my dear niece! What a story you must have for me!"

CHAPTER 4

"Oh, Aunt!" Lydia cried with a dramatic flourish, her eyes sparkling mischievously. "You should have seen Lizzy! She plunged headlong into the puddle like an ill-fated swallow, only to emerge a drenched and bedraggled creature indeed, coated from bonnet to hem in mud and muck!"

Lydia's vivid description sent a ripple of laughter through the gathered officers, their mirth amplified by the becoming flush that rose in Elizabeth's cheeks. "Lydia, you exaggerate!" she protested, her eyes narrowing at her sister's impertinence. "You were not even present to witness my unfortunate accident."

JANE ADELL

"No, but I saw everything through the window!" Lydia retorted with a triumphant grin, clearly relishing her role as a raconteur. "And you will not believe the best part, aunt. It all happened right before Mr. Darcy's very eyes!"

Elizabeth's face reddened further at the mention of Mr. Darcy. She could not help but cast a sidelong glance at Mr. Wickham, whose eyes sparkled with barely suppressed amusement.

Mr. Wickham stepped forward, his voice smooth and charming as ever. "Indeed, Mrs. Philips, your niece had an unfortunate misadventure due to the capricious weather, but it was our pleasure, my fellow officers and I, to provide assistance in her time of need."

He offered her a dashing smile, which the older woman returned with a coy flutter of her lashes. At the same time, the other officers agreed that coming to a young lady's aid was practically part of their militia duties.

Mrs. Philips clapped her hands together in delight. "Oh, I am so glad that such gallant gentlemen were nearby to come to her rescue." She surveyed the group of officers with an approving eye, her gaze lingering appreciatively on their handsome faces and resplendent uniforms.

As the group continued towards Longbourn, with their aunt who had turned around to join them, Mrs. Philips wasted no time in extracting every last detail of the day's events from the eager Lydia, her appetite for gossip insatiable. The officers, sensing an opportunity to impress the well-connected aunt, eagerly joined in the conversation, regaling her with tales of their own daring exploits and narrow escapes.

Elizabeth, meanwhile, found herself the unwilling center of attention, her sodden state serving as a constant reminder of her rather undignified tumble. Despite the light-hearted banter that surrounded her, she could not shake the image of Mr. Darcy's darkening countenance as he watched her walk away with Mr. Wickham. She smiled at the memory of his frustrated anger.

As they finally arrived at Longbourn, Mrs. Bennet, having been alerted to their arrival by a breathless servant, emerged from the house. Her eyes widened in shock at the sight of her disheveled daughter and the impressive retinue of officers accompanying her. She raised a hand to her chest, her voice shrill with alarm. "Oh, my poor Lizzy! What has befallen you?"

Before Elizabeth could attempt an explanation, Lydia leaped forward, her voice filled with dramatic flair. "Mama, it was the most extraordinary scene! Lizzy fell right—"

"Lydia, let us all inside first." Elizabeth interrupted her patience, wearing thin at another retelling of her misfortune. "I am sure the officers would love some refreshments after escorting us home."

"Yes, come in, come in! Hill will bring refreshments." As Elizabeth walked inside, Mrs. Bennet could not hide her dismay. "Mercy! What will become of your dress? Such a disaster!"

"It is only mud, Mama," Elizabeth replied with gentle exasperation. "I assure you, I shall recover."

As Elizabeth ascended the stairs to her room, she could not help but chuckle at the cacophony of voices that filled the parlor below. Her mother's shrill exhortations mingled with Lydia's boisterous laughter and the officers' exaggerated tales, creating a symphony of absurdity that was as familiar to her as it was exasperating. The sound followed her like a persistent echo as she closed the door behind her.

In the sanctuary of her chamber, Elizabeth took a moment to survey her disheveled appearance in the mirror. Mud streaked across her once-pristine gown like battle scars, a testament to her less-than-graceful encounter with the unforgiving mud puddle. With a wry smile, she began to remove the ruined fabric, her thoughts drifting to the events that had led her to this state.

The memory of Mr. Darcy's stormy expression as he watched her walk away with Mr. Wickham, sent an unexpected thrill down her spine. It seemed odd that such a reserved, prideful man could be so visibly affected by her association with another. Was it possible that Mr. Darcy felt something more than disdain for her?

She shook her head, dismissing the notion as fanciful nonsense. The very idea that the haughty Mr. Darcy could regard her with anything other than contempt was laughable. And yet, his reaction to Mr. Wickham had been unmistakable.

As she changed into a clean dress, Elizabeth wondered what had sparked such animosity between the two men. Mr. Wickham had shared a tale of woe, painting Mr. Darcy as a cruel oppressor who had denied him his rightful inheritance. But then why was Mr. Darcy angry at Mr. Wickham? Or was there another side to the story that she had yet to uncover?

Once properly attired and the initial excitement having subsided, Elizabeth descended the stairs, entered the room, and found herself seated beside Mr. Wickham, who engaged her in conversation with his usual wit and charm.

Mr. Wickham regaled her with amusing anecdotes of his military experiences, as well as stories from his childhood growing up near Pemberley. Elizabeth listened attentively, her curiosity piqued by these glimpses into his and Mr. Darcy's past.

As the visit wore on, she periodically observed Mr. Wickham's interactions with the other guests. He was undoubtedly popular, winning over even the most reserved among them with his affable demeanor and captivating presence.

"Come now, everyone!" Lydia exclaimed, clapping her hands together in excitement. "Let us play a game of charades! It will be a grand way to pass the time!"

"Capital idea, Lydia!" cried one of the officers, his good humor shining through. "I shall be on your team, of course!"

The room erupted into laughter and lively debates as the players began to arrange themselves into teams.

The game commenced with much enthusiasm, the teams taking turns acting out various scenes. One of the officers, in his usual boastful manner, exclaimed, "I am confident in my abilities to decipher any scene presented to me!"

During one of the rounds, Mr. Wickham, acting as a fearsome pirate, swaggered about the room with a makeshift eyepatch, causing the ladies to dissolve into fits of laughter.

"Is it Blackbeard?" cried Kitty, her eyes twinkling with mirth.

"No, no, it must be Captain Kidd!" Lydia chimed in, laughing heartily at Mr. Wickham's antics.

@@@

"You must concede," Mr. Bingley began, a note of mirth in his rich voice as he expertly guided his chestnut stallion down the dappled country lane, "the image of Miss Elizabeth besmirched in mud is quite an extraordinary sight for a lady of her standing."

Mr. Darcy's jaw tensed involuntarily, though he could not precisely discern why. Perhaps it was due to their impending arrival at Longbourn, where dashing officers were likely vying for Elizabeth's affections. "It was an accident," he responded curtly, his voice as crisp as the autumn air. "And I am certain she is mortified by the entire ordeal. We ought not to indulge in idle gossip."

"Of course not," replied Mr. Bingley, unable to suppress the mischievous grin that danced upon his lips. "It merely speaks to her indomitable spirit that she can weather such an event with her customary grace and good humor. But you must admit, Darcy, there is something comical in the situation."

Mr. Darcy grunted noncommittally, his steely gaze fixed on the horizon, unwilling to concede the point. In truth, the thought of Elizabeth stirred a warmth within him that threatened to dismantle his carefully constructed defenses. He could not deny the magnetic pull she had on him; indeed, the mere suggestion of her in the company of Mr. Wickham had been enough to set his blood aflame.

As they approached the stately facade of Longbourn, the strains of raucous laughter emanating from within served only to fan the flames of jealousy licking at his insides. Mr. Darcy steeled himself for the encounter ahead, determined to maintain his composure in the face of this maddening attraction Elizabeth seemed to have for that worthless rogue.

With practiced ease, Mr. Bingley flashed a genial smile at his friend, though it did not quite touch the depths of his eyes. "It appears, Darcy, that we have arrived just in time for a rather spirited gathering."

Mr. Darcy offered a curt nod, his visage inscrutable as he gracefully dismounted his ebony steed. His gloved hand rapped firmly on the door, the sound barely audible above the cacophony of merriment within. Eventually, they were ushered into the resplendent foyer by a servant whose announcement of their arrival was entirely drowned out by the boisterous laughter echoing from the drawing room.

His smoldering gaze lingered on Elizabeth, ensconced beside Mr. Wickham, their heads bent together in intimate conversation. The sight only served to stoke the simmering ire within him as tendrils of jealousy coiled around his heart.

CHAPTER 5

Mrs. Bennet finally noticed their arrival and hurried towards them, her voice a blend of surprise and delight. "Why, Mr. Bingley! You are very, very welcome." Her tone turned frosty as she added, "And Mr. Darcy. You are welcome too."

Mr. Darcy's posture remained rigid and formal, his jaw set in a tight line as he acknowledged Mrs. Bennet's greeting with a curt nod.

Mr. Bingley could not help but cast an anxious glance toward Jane, whose attention had been captured by one of the officers. To his consternation, she had not yet observed his entrance. She was still engrossed in conversation with a man seated beside her.

"Ah, gentlemen," said Mr. Bingley, his voice lilting over the ensuing silence with practiced grace, "we apologize for interrupting your merriment. We simply wished to inquire after Miss Elizabeth's well-being, following her... unfortunate mishap in town."

At this, the rest of the room began to take notice of the unexpected arrivals. The lively game of charades they had been immersed in came to a sudden halt as all eyes swiveled from the newcomers to Elizabeth, whose cheeks bloomed like roses.

She briefly met Mr. Darcy's gaze before addressing Mr. Bingley with a radiant smile. "Thank you, sir, for your kind inquiry. I assure you, I have quite recovered from my embarrassment and suffered no ill effects."

This appeared to satisfy Mr. Bingley, who grinned warmly at her response. Jane allowed herself a small, knowing smile directed at Mr. Bingley, making his smile grow even more dazzling under her tender gaze.

Mrs. Bennet clapped her hands together, drawing everyone's attention. "Now that we have some additional players let us rearrange the teams for our game of charades."

She could barely contain her delight as she announced, "Mr. Bingley, you shall join my dear Jane's team." Jane blushed a delicate pink, casting a shy glance towards Mr. Bingley, who beamed at her with genuine affection.

Just as it seemed Mr. Darcy might be the odd man out, Lydia chimed in, her voice teasingly playful. "Oh, but what about poor Mary in the corner? Surely, she would enjoy joining in the fun as well!"

Mrs. Bennet seized upon this opportunity to pair them together, exclaiming, "That's an excellent idea, Lydia. Mr. Darcy, you shall join Mary's team."

All eyes turned to Mr. Darcy with bated breath as a soft ripple of amusement passed through the room. Even Elizabeth felt the corner of her mouth twitch at the prospect.

Ever mindful of his manners and the expectations of a gentleman, Mr. Darcy nodded stiffly, "Very well, I shall join Miss Mary's team."

His partnership with Mary might even serve as a welcome distraction from the disquieting emotions that had plagued him throughout the evening.

Mary sat with a mixture of shock and delight etched upon her plain features. She hesitated only a moment before rising from her seat and making her way to join the group, stealing furtive glances at the imposing figure of Mr. Darcy as they assembled themselves into teams.

He found himself unable to resist stealing glances at Elizabeth, noting how her eyes seemed to flicker with an unspoken challenge whenever they met his own. The tension between them crackled like a hidden current, lending a sense of exhilaration to the proceedings.

During the game, he attempted to conceal his discomfort and focus on performing his role to the best of his abilities. He maintained a stoic expression as he acted out his charades with a dignified air. On the other hand, Mr. Bingley's performance during the charades was nothing short of enchanting, eliciting laughter and applause from the gathered company.

Mr. Darcy could not help but acknowledge the undeniable chemistry between his friend and Jane as she basked in the adoring attention, their connection evident through their shared theatrics.

Mr. Wickham excelled at presenting the image of a perfect gentleman, engaging in lighthearted banter, and winning over the hearts of many. This only heightened Mr. Darcy's frustration, who was all too familiar with Wickham's true nature. He did his best to hide his discomfort and focus on performing his role in the game while keeping a watchful eye on his nemesis.

It was not until Elizabeth took her turn at the center of the game, acting out a scene from Romeo and Juliet with a fervor that would have impressed even the most seasoned thespian, that Mr. Darcy's icy reserve began to thaw. His eyes never left her movements — the grace and animation with which she conveyed each wordless clue, her laughter infectious.

So it was that Mr. Darcy found himself grudgingly participating, driven by the desire to match Elizabeth's intellect and spirit in this spirited contest and outshine Mr. Wickham's performance. When it was once again his turn, he took a deep breath, steeling himself for the task ahead, and to the astonishment of all present, launched into an impressive display of pantomime.

At first, there was silence – a collective holding of breath as the partygoers watched in disbelief as the stoic Mr. Darcy performed with unexpected gusto. And then, slowly, laughter began to fill the room as the others recognized the humor in such an incongruous sight.

As the game ended and the teams disbanded, Mr. Darcy met Elizabeth's gaze from across the room. For once, it held no trace of disdain or judgment but rather a warmth, a shared amusement that spoke volumes about the subtle shift that had occurred between them.

Captain Carter addressed the room with a touch of regret. "Ladies and gentlemen, it is with great sadness that we must bid you adieu for the evening. Our duties call upon us to attend elsewhere."

This sent a ripple of disappointment throughout the room as each participant in the game set about offering their heartfelt farewells. Mr. Wickham, ever the charmer, leaned towards Elizabeth with a roguish grin. "Miss Elizabeth, it is my deepest regret that I must take my leave now, especially when I would much rather linger in the enchanting presence of a lady such as yourself," he said, his words dripping with unctuous charm.

Elizabeth met his gaze, a playful twinkle in her eyes as she replied, "Mr. Wickham, your flattery is most generous. However, we do understand that duty calls and cannot be ignored. We shall look forward to your next visit with anticipation and hope that it will be just as delightful as this evening has been."

Lt. Denny bowed before Jane, "I cannot express how much we have enjoyed your company tonight. It has been an evening to remember."

"Thank you ever so kindly," Jane replied with a gracious smile, her eyes shining with genuine warmth. "Your presence has indeed transformed this into a most delightful evening, and we shall eagerly anticipate any future occasions where we may have the pleasure of your esteemed company."

Lydia chimed in playfully, twirling a dark curl around her finger as she batted her eyelashes at Lt.

Denny. "We shall miss you terribly, sir! Pray, promise us you will visit again, anon!"

"Fear not, Miss Lydia," he replied gallantly, a mischievous glint in his eyes. "For I am certain that we shall return ere long and with renewed vigor for more amusing diversions."

Amidst the chaos of parting gestures and exchanged pleasantries, Mr. Darcy seized his opportunity. He moved with quiet determination towards Elizabeth, the intensity of his gaze never faltering. As he drew near, he addressed her in an almost inaudible murmur, "Miss Elizabeth, might I have a word with you in private?"

Elizabeth, caught off guard by the suddenness of his request, hesitated for a moment before nodding her assent. They slipped away from the boisterous crowd and into the relative sanctuary of a far corner of the room, where the cacophony of voices served to provide a veil of privacy over their conversation.

He wasted no time in coming to the point. "I must warn you, Miss Elizabeth, of the grave danger posed by your association with Mr. Wickham. He is not the man he appears to be."

Skepticism flickered across Elizabeth's features as she regarded him carefully. "What reason do I have to believe that your judgment is sound?"

Her doubt galled him, but he pressed on, swallowing his pride as he spoke in hushed tones. "Miss Elizabeth, you must understand that my concern is not born of jealousy but rather out of genuine apprehension for your safety. Wickham's true character is one of deception and duplicity, concealed beneath a charming façade."

Elizabeth arched a brow, her expression guarded. "You paint a rather dark picture of the man, Mr. Darcy. I have observed nothing but amiability and charm in Mr. Wickham's character."

Mr. Darcy straightened his posture, struggling to articulate the urgency he felt without violating the reserves of propriety. "I assure you, Miss Elizabeth, my words come from a place of experience and honest observation. I have known Mr. Wickham since our boyhood and have witnessed firsthand the depths of his deceit. He has caused irrevocable harm to those around him, all the while maintaining an air of innocence and charisma."

Elizabeth's lips pursed as she considered his words, her eyes narrowing just slightly. "It seems our experiences have been quite different, Mr. Darcy. Until I have evidence to the contrary, I shall continue to regard Mr. Wickham as a gentleman and a friend."

Mr. Darcy's frustration mounted, his jaw clenching with the strain of withholding the entirety of Wickham's perfidy. The very air between them began to crackle with tension. "Miss Elizabeth," he began, desperation lacing his voice, "I implore you to trust me in this matter. I..." He broke off, clearly wrestling with himself before continuing. "I beseech you not to reveal what I am about to tell you to another living soul."

Elizabeth, curiosity piqued by the promise of revelation, leaned in ever so slightly. "Very well, Mr. Darcy. I swear to hold your confidence."

With a hesitant breath, Mr. Darcy delved into the sordid tale. "He once attempted to elope with my sister, who was but fifteen years of age."

The revelation struck Elizabeth like a thunderbolt, leaving her momentarily breathless as she struggled to assimilate this new information into her understanding of Mr. Wickham's character. A myriad of emotions played across her expressive face – disbelief, shock, and finally, a budding sense of betrayal.

"Your sister?" she echoed, the words tasting bitter on her tongue as she grappled with the implications of his confession.

"Yes," Mr. Darcy confirmed grimly, his gaze unwavering. "Georgiana barely escaped severe consequences. She was not the only unmarried gentlewoman he had pursued, but in my sister's case, thankfully, she confessed all to me the day they were to elope." He paused for a moment, allowing the weight of his words to sink in before continuing. "I had been deceived by my sister's governess, who had been a longstanding paramour of his. I beseech you; distance yourself from that man. He is not worthy of your trust nor your esteem. All of this can be verified by my cousin Col. Fitzwilliam, who shares guardianship of my sister."

His impassioned plea hung heavy in the air between them, underscored by the muted echoes of laughter and conversation that filtered from the other side of the room.

Finally, she lifted her chin, her expression resolute. "Thank you, Mr. Darcy, for your candor. I shall …

take your words under advisement." She hesitated for a moment, meeting his intense gaze with her own. "And I shall be more cautious in my dealings with Mr. Wickham."

Relief washed over Mr. Darcy's features, softening the hard lines of his visage. "I am grateful that you have chosen to consider my warning," he said quietly, his voice laden with sincerity.

CHAPTER 6

Elizabeth sought refuge in the sanctuary of her chamber following Mr. Darcy's startling revelations, as she found it difficult to digest the magnitude of his confession. The evening's events swirled tumultuously in her thoughts like a tempestuous wind, stirring up emotions she scarcely understood.

As the door to their shared room creaked open, Elizabeth glanced up to find Jane entering, her cheeks flushed and her eyes alight with excitement. "Lizzy," she began breathlessly, "I have been searching for you everywhere!"

"Oh, Jane," Elizabeth sighed, the burdensome weight of the evening's revelations pressing down upon her like a millstone. "I have so much to tell you."

Alerted by the distress in her sister's tone, Jane immediately set aside her embroidery. She gestured for Elizabeth to sit beside her on the cushioned window seat. "What is it, Lizzy? You seem quite unsettled," she said, her brow furrowing in genuine concern.

Elizabeth hesitated, wrestling with her promise to maintain Mr. Darcy's confidence. How could she balance loyalty to him with the need to protect her family from Wickham's machinations? Finally, she resolved to tell Jane just enough to warn her of the potential danger they faced.

"It is regarding Mr. Wickham," Elizabeth began cautiously, choosing her words carefully. "Mr. Darcy confided in me this evening that he believes Wickham to be a deceitful and dangerous man."

The shock that crossed Jane's countenance was all too evident. Her eyes widened, and her lips parted as she struggled to comprehend this jarring notion. "But how can that be, Lizzy? He has always been so pleasant and agreeable in our company."

With a sigh, Elizabeth elaborated as much as she dared, relating Mr. Darcy's insistence that his concerns were based on personal experience and long-standing knowledge of Wickham's character. She stopped short of revealing the particulars of his sister's near-elopement, trusting that Jane would understand the gravity of the situation without requiring explicit detail.

When she had finished, Jane shook her head in disbelief. "Oh, Lizzy, this is most distressing news. What are we to do? Surely we must inform Mama and Papa."

Elizabeth bit her lip in consternation. "It is a delicate matter, Jane. While I agree that our parents should be made aware, I fear that Mama, in her characteristic enthusiasm, may inadvertently disclose the information to others, thus causing irreparable harm to Mr. Darcy's sister."

Jane considered this predicament carefully, her brow furrowed in thought. "Perhaps, then, it would be best to confide only in Papa. I trust he will be able to take appropriate measures to shield Lydia from Wickham without alerting Mama to the entire truth."

Nodding in agreement, Elizabeth felt a small measure of relief as they devised their plan. Relieved by their decision, she felt the weight upon her chest momentarily lift. "Oh, Jane," Elizabeth began with a playful smile, "I have been so caught up in my own affairs that I have neglected to ask after yours. How did you find playing charades this evening, especially with a certain charming partner?"

A becoming blush rose on Jane's cheeks. "Mr. Bingley was a most agreeable companion for the game. He has a quick wit and lively sense of humor that quite matched my own."

"I am certain he found your wit and humor equally diverting," Elizabeth teased. Her spirits lifted further at the sparkle of joy in Jane's eyes.

Jane sighed dreamily before hesitantly adding, "And were you not surprised at Mr. Darcy's performance this evening? I would never have imagined him enjoying such an amusement, let alone acting with such enthusiasm."

Elizabeth's grin widened. Her own astonishment echoed in Jane's observation. "You are quite right. His final charade was particularly masterful. For one typically so reserved, it seems charades brings out his inner showman."

They shared a giggle at the peculiarity of the notion. As their laughter faded, Elizabeth sighed and then glanced at Jane. "I shall speak with Papa now about Mr. Darcy's revelations. I think it is best to address this matter as soon as possible."

Jane nodded in understanding, her eyes filled with concern. "Yes, Lizzy, it is important that we act swiftly."

Descending the staircase, Elizabeth passed by Lydia and Kitty, who were still laughing heartily and mimicking some of the most exaggerated expressions from their evening of charades. The sight brought a small smile to her face as she admired their carefree spirits, determined to keep them safe.

As Elizabeth approached the study, she paused to collect her thoughts before knocking softly on the door. A muffled voice granted her entry, and she found Mr. Bennet sitting behind his desk, a thick book open before him and the remnants of a small glass of port at his side.

"Ah, Lizzy," he said, peering over his spectacles. "I am glad to see you. The raucous noise from your sisters' merriment has finally lessened. I was beginning to fear the walls themselves might shake loose from their foundations." His wry smile met her eyes, but it failed to alleviate the seriousness of her purpose.

"Indeed, Papa," she replied, taking a seat across from him. "But I must speak with you about a matter of great importance."

Mr. Bennet closed his book, his expression sobering as he regarded his favorite daughter intently. "Very well, Lizzy, what is it?"

Elizabeth took a deep breath and recounted Mr. Darcy's warnings about Mr. Wickham. As she spoke, Mr. Bennet listened attentively, his brow furrowing with concern. When she finished, she looked at him expectantly, awaiting his reaction.

For several moments, Mr. Bennet was silent, lost in thought. Finally, he sighed and shook his head. "Lizzy, Mr. Darcy is a powerful man, and his opinion should not be taken lightly. However, I find it difficult to believe that Mr. Wickham is as dangerous as he claims. Could it be that Mr. Darcy is merely attempting to keep you from Mr. Wickham due to jealousy?"

Elizabeth's cheeks flushed at the insinuation. "I assure you, Papa, Mr. Darcy has no reason to be jealous. He has not the slightest inclination to court me, and we will never be anything more than mere acquaintances."

Her father raised an eyebrow. "Very well, but consider this: if Mr. Wickham is truly a scoundrel, why would he present himself in our society, knowing full well that his misdeeds might be uncovered? It seems a rather reckless course of action."

Elizabeth nodded thoughtfully, conceding that her father had a point. She couldn't shake the conviction that Mr. Darcy's words held truth. "Papa, I understand your perspective, but I cannot ignore the possibility that Mr. Wickham poses a threat to our family if not all the young women of Meryton."

Mr. Bennet regarded her carefully before nodding. "Very well, Lizzy. I trust your judgment, and I will keep a watchful eye on Mr. Wickham. But remember my dear, there are always two sides to every story. Let us not forget that even the most upstanding gentlemen can have their secrets."

With that cryptic statement, Mr. Bennet returned to his book, signaling the end of their discussion.

Elizabeth left the study feeling somewhat reassured yet still troubled that Mr. Wickham could ensnare her younger sisters, for Mr. Bennet notoriously avoided assemblies and other social gatherings if he could.

∽

As THE EVENING meal at Netherfield unfolded, Mr. Darcy sat ensconced at the opulent table adorned with gold-rimmed plates and crystal goblets, his attention torn between the exquisite culinary offerings laid before him and the animated conversation that ebbed and flowed around him like a babbling brook. The tantalizing aroma of succulent roasted meats and warm, fresh-baked bread wafted through the air, teasing his senses as he endeavored to concentrate on the fare before him; however, the vivacious discourse between his friends and acquaintances presented an increasingly formidable distraction.

Mr. Bingley, with bright eyes and infectious enthusiasm, regaled his sisters with spirited accounts of the delightful afternoon spent in the company of the Bennets at Longbourn. "I must say," he effused, "the charades we partook in were nothing short of captivating! I have never experienced anything quite so enjoyable in all my days."

Caroline Bingley and Louisa Hurst exchanged disapproving glances, their genteel expressions carefully schooled in disdain, before Louisa replied in a voice dripping with icy condescension, "How utterly quaint, Charles. Such parlor games might amuse those unaccustomed to society's more refined pleasures. Still, I confess I find them rather... pedestrian."

Caroline nodded her assent, her delicate features alighting in a smug smile. "Indeed, I'm certain our esteemed Mr. Darcy would never deign to engage in such infantile diversions." She cast an expectant glance in his direction, awaiting confirmation of her assertion.

A faint blush suffused Mr. Darcy's cheeks under Caroline's anticipatory gaze. Yet, he maintained his composure, taking a slow, deliberate sip of the ruby-red wine before responding in a measured tone, "On the contrary, Miss Bingley, I did, in fact, partake in the charades this very afternoon."

Exchanging astonished glances, Caroline and Louisa's perfectly arched eyebrows ascended towards their expertly coiffed tresses. Evidently, they had not anticipated such a candid admission from their esteemed companion.

"In truth," Mr. Darcy continued, a semblance of amusement infusing his voice, "I found myself fortuitously partnered with none other than Miss Mary Bennet."

Gasps reverberated around the room as though he had divulged some scandalous secret. The sisters gaped at him in utter disbelief, their faces blanching with shock. Mr. Bingley, however, grinned broadly, clearly reveling in the discomfiture of his sisters.

"But surely," stammered Caroline, striving to regain her poise, "your participation must have been motivated by politeness rather than genuine enjoyment of such... pastimes?"

With a wry smile playing at the corners of his lips, Mr. Darcy addressed her unspoken insinuation. "While it is indeed true that a gentleman must comport himself accordingly in all situations, I cannot deny that I found the experience... illuminating."

Candelabras flickered, casting sinuous shadows upon the walls as the sisters grappled with this unforeseen revelation.

Mr. Hurst, who had hitherto remained silent and thoroughly engrossed in the consumption of a succulent leg of roast chicken, glanced up with greasy fingers and interjected his own prosaic contribution to the conversation.

"You know what would render charades infinitely more pleasurable?" he opined, seemingly oblivious to the prevailing tension in the chamber. "A wager – or perhaps the consolation of a glass or two of fine brandy for the vanquished party!"

Peals of laughter echoed through the room at his ludicrous proposal, affording Mr. Darcy a welcome reprieve from the scrutiny he had lately endured. As the conversation meandered towards other subjects, such as the latest modish fashions and the prospects of the impending hunting season, Mr. Darcy's gaze inadvertently strayed to the window, which framed the glittering stars and the silvern gardens beyond.

A sudden yearning for an evening promenade seized him – one that might, perchance, culminate in an encounter with a certain quick-witted, vivacious, and intelligent young woman whose visage was never far from his thoughts.

CHAPTER 7

The following day found the Bennet sisters strolling through Meryton, their eyes entranced by the shop windows that boasted an array of ribbons and trinkets promising delight. The fragrant scent of blossoms carried on a gentle breeze as they walked while the warm sun cast flickering shadows from the trees upon their path.

Elizabeth walked in tandem with Jane, her brow furrowed, and lips pursed with concern. "Jane, I cannot help but feel disquieted regarding Papa's reaction. He seems far too nonchalant about the threat Mr. Wickham poses," Elizabeth confessed softly, her voice barely audible above the rustle of their skirts.

Jane, however, appeared preoccupied, her gaze scanning the bustling streets in hopes of catching a glimpse of Mr. Bingley. "Yes, Lizzy, I understand your unease, but perhaps Papa is right to reserve judgment until further evidence presents itself."

As they conversed, the familiar sight of the militia officers emerged from around a corner, their crimson uniforms drawing the attention of all who passed. Lydia and Kitty squealed and hastened to join the young men, leaving Elizabeth, Jane, and Mary behind.

Elizabeth regarded Mr. Wickham with newfound wariness, his charm now overshadowed by Mr. Darcy's revelations. As he chatted animatedly with her younger sisters, Mr. Wickham's furtive glances betrayed his concern as he excused himself from Lydia and Kitty to approach her.

"Miss Elizabeth," he began amiably, attempting to engage her in conversation. "I cannot help but notice that your reception of me today is rather... different. Have I done something to offend you?"

She hesitated, then decided on a more indirect line of inquiry. "Tell me, Mr. Wickham, do you happen to know a Col. Fitzwilliam?"

Mr. Wickham's expression flickered momentarily, betraying his surprise at the unexpected question before he regained composure. "No, I am afraid I am not acquainted with the gentleman."

Elizabeth regarded him intently, her suspicions piqued by his reaction. "Are you certain? He is a cousin of Mr. Darcy, after all, and I thought perhaps you might have met him during your time at Pemberley."

He hesitated again before replying, "Ah, yes, now that you mention it, I do recall the name. Col. Fitzwilliam must have visited Pemberley when I was but a child. Our paths have not crossed since then." He smiled charmingly and then asked, "What makes you inquire about that person? Did you have a conversation with Mr. Darcy? Are you confidants now?" He teasingly said.

Elizabeth attempted to deflect his probing. "The matter simply came up in passing. But it seems you are rather interested in what Mr. Darcy may have told me."

"Perhaps," Wickham admitted cautiously, "but that is only because I wish to ensure that you are not unduly influenced by his version of events."

Feeling cornered, Elizabeth donned a smile and replied, "Well, Mr. Wickham, I do appreciate your concern, but I assure you, I am quite capable of forming my own opinions. However, I must excuse myself now. I have the important duty of saving my younger sisters from depleting their pin money on frivolous purchases."

"Oh, do not worry too much about them, Miss Elizabeth," Wickham said with a teasing grin. "Surely the enjoyment they derive from such purchases outweighs the potential harm."

Elizabeth's eyes sparkled with a hint of amusement as she retorted, "That may be true, Mr. Wickham, but it is the responsibility of the elder sister to ensure some semblance of prudence in the spending habits of her younger siblings. Otherwise, they might not have any pin money left for more important occasions."

With that, she curtsied and turned away, leaving Mr. Wickham to ponder their exchange. Her heart raced with the knowledge that she had just witnessed the mask slip, revealing the cunning and deceitful man that Mr. Darcy had warned her about.

With a resolute air, Elizabeth approached Lydia and Kitty, announcing that they would be paying a visit to their Aunt Philips. At Lydia's protest that they had just called upon her recently, Elizabeth shushed her sister. She gently steered them in the direction of their aunt's residence.

As the sisters turned to leave, Elizabeth caught Mr. Wickham's gaze, and she could see the curiosity in his eyes. She hoped that her actions hadn't aroused his suspicions but knew that distancing her sisters from him was the prudent course to take.

Upon arriving at Mrs. Philips' home, the girls were drawn into a conversation about the handsome officers stationed in Meryton. However, Elizabeth's thoughts were elsewhere, her mind preoccupied with the realization that Mr. Darcy had been right about Mr. Wickham all along.

As they sipped tea and exchanged pleasantries, Elizabeth struggled to hide her anxiety from her family. She knew she must speak with Mr. Bennet once more to insist on his intervention regarding Mr. Wickham, but how could she convey the urgency without revealing too much?

When it was time to leave, Elizabeth linked arms with Jane as they walked back to Longbourn. As they strolled through the picturesque countryside, Elizabeth recounted her recent encounter with Mr. Wickham, detailing his evasiveness and apparent attempts to manipulate her opinion of Mr. Darcy.

"I believe it is clear now that Mr. Darcy was telling the truth," she confided in Jane. "We must speak with Papa again to ensure he takes appropriate action."

Jane appeared torn between disbelief and concern, her brow furrowed as she contemplated the implications of what Elizabeth had shared. "I find it difficult to accept that Mr. Wickham has behaved so duplicitously, Lizzy," she admitted hesitantly. "Throughout our acquaintance, he has demonstrated nothing but the manners of a gentleman."

Elizabeth sighed, understanding her sister's reluctance to condemn a man they had all found charming and agreeable. "Indeed, Jane, it is a most distressing realization. But we cannot ignore the evidence before us nor the potential danger he poses to our family."

"You are right, Lizzy. We must ensure Papa takes this matter seriously and does what is necessary to protect us all." Jane nodded slowly, her expression solemn as she acknowledged the gravity of the situation.

~

ELIZABETH ENTERED the study of Longbourn, her steps firm and determined as she sought out her father. Mr. Bennet sat in his favorite armchair by the window, pouring over a large volume with studious attention.

"Papa," Elizabeth began, her voice clear and resolute. "I must insist on speaking with you about Mr. Wickham once more."

Mr. Bennet looked up from his book, a faint smile playing at the corners of his mouth as he observed his second daughter's resolute expression. "Ah, Lizzy, your pertinacity is truly something to behold. Very well, what new information do you have to present?"

Elizabeth recounted her conversation with Mr. Wickham, emphasizing his reaction to Colonel Fitzwilliam's name and his evasiveness when questioned about their connection. As she spoke, she noticed her father's eyes narrowing, the hint of amusement disappearing from his countenance.

"Nevertheless, Lizzy," Mr. Bennet said after she had finished her tale, "it could simply be that Mr. Wickham was reminded of someone else entirely when you mentioned Colonel Fitzwilliam. You know, coincidences are not uncommon in our world."

"Papa!" Elizabeth exclaimed, her exasperation barely contained. "Surely, you cannot dismiss this evidence so lightly! I fear what he may do, especially given Lydia's propensity to flirt with the officers."

Mr. Bennet heaved a forlorn sigh, gently placing the leather-bound book he had been engrossed in onto the polished wooden table before pinching the bridge of his nose. "My dear child," he began, his voice laden with weary affection, "Lydia will persist in being Lydia, regardless of the proximity of any officers. There can be no harm that arises from it. We are well-regarded in the neighborhood, and none would permit Mr. Wickham to act impetuously toward our daughters. Moreover, whenever they enjoy each other's company, others are always present. I beseech you, do not burden yourself with baseless trepidations, Lizzy."

Elizabeth clasped her hands together, frustration simmering within her like water on the verge of boiling. How could her father remain so impervious to the potential peril lurking beneath Mr. Wickham's beguiling facade? She bit her lip, endeavoring to restrain her emotions as she contemplated her subsequent course of action.

"Very well, Papa," she yielded, her voice taut with strain. "I shall place my trust in your judgment, although I cannot dispel this disquiet that plagues me."

Mr. Bennet tenderly patted his daughter's hand, offering a reassuring smile. "Lizzy, my dear, you have always relied on your instincts, and I harbor no doubts as to their merit. We shall maintain our vigilance, but let us refrain from allowing our imaginations to run amok."

With that, Elizabeth inclined her head in acquiescence, accepting her father's words for the moment. But as she withdrew from Mr. Bennet's study, her thoughts consumed by the enigmatic Mr. Wickham, she silently vowed to unravel the truth, whatever it may entail, and safeguard her family from any misfortune that might befall them.

An uproar in the hallway roused Elizabeth from her ruminations, the clamor of raised voices and spirited chatter seeping through the corridor from the drawing room. Her curiosity piqued, she stepped into the room and was greeted by the sight of Mr. Bingley and his sister Caroline standing just inside the entrance, encircled by her family. The color had suffused Jane's cheeks as she averted her gaze, evidently discomposed by Mr. Bingley's unrelenting stare.

"My dear Bennets," Mr. Bingley commenced, his voice brimming with jovial warmth, "I am elated to extend an invitation to each of you to attend a ball at Netherfield Park this forthcoming Friday evening."

Caroline Bingley, the very epitome of sophistication and grace, chimed in with a taut smile, "We do hope you will honor us with your esteemed presence."

Mrs. Bennet appeared oblivious to any frostiness emanating from Miss Bingley as she clapped her hands together in delight. "A ball! How utterly splendid! Of course, we shall attend, Mr. Bingley!"

The remainder of the family murmured their assent, with Lydia and Kitty practically vibrating on their heels in anticipation. "Oh, how marvelous!" Lydia exclaimed. "Just think of all the officers who will be in attendance!"

Kitty chimed in eagerly, "Indeed, and perchance there will be new gentlemen for us to meet as well!"

Even Mary seemed mildly intrigued, though she made an effort to appear nonchalant about the upcoming event. "While dancing may not be my preferred pastime," she said, adjusting her spectacles, "I must concede that the prospect of attending another ball is not entirely displeasing."

Throughout the exchange, Mr. Bingley's eyes remained steadfastly locked on Jane, a mixture of warmth and affection radiating brilliantly within them. Elizabeth couldn't help but smile softly at the tender scene, feeling her sister's happiness as if it were her own.

As the Bingleys took their leave, Elizabeth observed her sisters' mounting excitement. Plans for dresses, ribbons, and suitable dancing partners swirled in the air as they hastened to prepare for the forthcoming festivities.

Amidst the flurry of activity, Elizabeth couldn't help but feel a thrill of anticipation herself, although it was tempered by a shadow of uncertainty. She knew that Mr. Darcy would also be present at the ball. After their heated encounters, the prospect of confronting him again filled her with a mélange of trepidation and intrigue.

"Girls!" Mrs. Bennet exclaimed, her eyes alight with exhilaration. "We must attend to your dresses for the ball posthaste! You know you desire to appear your finest for the officers, and we ought to secure our ribbons and trinkets before the Lucases lay claim to them all."

Elizabeth sighed inwardly, resigning herself to the fact that a leisurely walk was now out of the question. The notion of spending the afternoon in Meryton amongst the officers – particularly Mr. Wickham – was far from enticing.

Mary glanced up from her pianoforte practice, which she had commenced immediately following the Bingleys' departure, most likely in preparation for an exhibition at the upcoming ball. "I am more than capable of assisting with the dress alterations, Mama," she proffered hesitantly. "But I fear I will not have sufficient time to complete them all before the ball."

Mrs. Bennet waved her hand dismissively. "No, no, my dear. We shall venture into Meryton and engage the services of a seamstress to ensure everything is impeccable."

"But Mama," Elizabeth interjected, endeavoring to dissuade her mother from this course of action that would place them squarely in the path of the officers once more, "Perhaps it would be best if we postponed our visit to the seamstress until tomorrow morning?"

Mrs. Bennet huffed, her impatience evident as she retorted, "If we tarry, we shall find ourselves at the mercy of the Lucases and their cunning ways. They will snatch up all the finest ribbons and adornments, leaving naught for us."

Elizabeth tried again. "By the time we arrive in Meryton, the shops are likely to be closed anyway. The afternoon is waning, and we can depart first thing in the morning, ensuring that we have our choice of the most exquisite materials before anyone else."

Mrs. Bennet nodded reluctantly, seemingly mollified by Elizabeth's reasoning. "Very well," she acquiesced, "we shall leave early tomorrow morning. But mark my words, girls, you must be prepared to make swift decisions. We cannot afford to dawdle or permit the Lucases to outshine us at the ball."

With that, Elizabeth breathed a sigh of relief, grateful for the reprieve from Meryton's bustling streets and Mr. Wickham's disquieting presence.

∽

THE FOLLOWING MORNING, the Bennet sisters and their mother set out for Meryton, their spirits buoyed by the prospect of acquiring the ribbons and embellishments for their gowns.

"So, dear sister, have you thought about which gown you shall don at the ball? I presume it shall be the one that best showcases your figure?" Elizabeth asked with a sly grin.

Jane blushed slightly, her cheeks turning a delicate shade of pink. "Oh, Lizzy, you know I do not pay particular attention to such matters very well. But I must admit, I am rather partial to my blue silk gown."

Elizabeth giggled as they continued on their way, feeling a surge of sisterly affection. Their conversation soon turned to other subjects, but the undercurrent of excitement surrounding the forthcoming ball was ever-present.

Upon reaching Meryton, Mrs. Bennet wasted no time in ushering her daughters into the dressmaker's shop, eager to secure the most fashionable trims. To their collective dismay, however, the seamstress informed them that she was fully booked and unable to make alterations to their dresses in time for the Netherfield ball.

Crestfallen, Lydia, and Kitty pouted as they exited the shop, their dreams of wearing impeccably tailored gowns dashed. "It is simply unjust!" Lydia lamented while Kitty nodded vigorously in agreement.

With an air of resolute determination, Mrs. Bennet astutely concocted a new scheme. "We shall purchase our ribbons and embellishments at the milliner's shop and then return home to alter the dresses ourselves. Mary is proficient with a needle and thread, and I am sure we can manage between the lot of us."

A surprising stroke of luck ensured that they were not accosted by any of the dashing officers who usually strolled the streets of Meryton. Elizabeth couldn't help but feel relieved at this turn of events, grateful for the opportunity to avoid an uncomfortable encounter with Mr. Wickham.

CHAPTER 8

The following morning, as the Bennet family gathered 'round the breakfast table, sunlight filtering through the lace curtains and casting delicate patterns on their faces, Mr. Bennet captivated the room with an unexpected announcement. "Ladies," he began, a mischievous twinkle in his eye, "we shall have a guest joining us for dinner this evening."

Mrs. Bennet's eyes widened with excitement, her teacup rattling in its saucer as she exclaimed, "Oh, is it Mr. Bingley? How delightful!"

Mr. Bennet chuckled at his wife's enthusiasm, shaking his head. "No, my dear, not Mr. Bingley. We are to expect a visit from someone we have never met before, our distant cousin, Mr. Collins."

With a sigh that could move mountains, Mrs. Bennet lamented, "Oh, my dear, pray, do not mention that odious man. It is the hardest thing in the world that your estate should be entailed away from your poor children."

Mr. Bennet replied, his voice rich with irony, "Indeed, my dear, nothing can clear Mr. Collins of the iniquitous crime of inheriting Longbourn, but if you will listen to his letter, you may be softened by his manner of expressing himself."

As Mr. Bennet read aloud from the letter, it became apparent that Mr. Collins possessed a talent for grandiloquence that rivaled even the most seasoned of orators. His sentences were veritable labyrinths of pomp and circumstance, meandering through a landscape of obsequiousness and self-importance.

Elizabeth couldn't help but exchange amused glances with her sister Jane as their father continued to recite the missive. The absurdity of Mr. Collins' effusive praise for his patroness, Lady Catherine de Bourgh, was only matched by his ability to weave into every sentence a reminder of his own humble position as her lowly clergyman.

"And so, dear cousin," Mr. Bennet concluded, folding the letter and tucking it back into its envelope, "Mr. Collins wishes to extend the olive branch of reconciliation and hopes that his visit will be the beginning of a renewed friendship between our two families."

Lydia, ever eager to interject her opinion, chimed in without hesitation. "He sounds dreadfully dull! I do hope he'll bring some handsome young men with him to make up for it."

The remainder of the day passed in a flurry of activity as the Bennet household prepared for the arrival of their esteemed visitor. Elizabeth found herself torn between amusement and irritation at the prospect of entertaining Mr. Collins; she anticipated that his presence would provide ample fodder for her wit.

That evening, Mr. Collins arrived and proved to be every bit as ridiculous as Mr. Bennet had anticipated. It became increasingly apparent that Mr. Collins possessed an almost supernatural ability to insert himself into every conversation, offering unsolicited advice and regaling the company with anecdotes of his illustrious patroness.

The Bennet sisters found themselves exchanging a series of discreet eye rolls and stifled giggles as they endured his pontifications. Despite their best efforts, the sisters struggled to maintain their composure as he prattled on, each exchange more absurd than the last.

Mr. Collins, after clearing his throat with an unnecessary level of pomp, stood up to address the room. "Ladies and gentlemen," he began, his voice lending an air of importance, "I have come to share a matter of great consequence with you."

The Bennet sisters exchanged wary glances as their mother looked on expectantly.

"My esteemed patroness, Lady Catherine de Bourgh – whom I am sure you all admire as much as I do – has given me her blessing in my search for a suitable wife," Mr. Collins announced, puffing out his chest with pride. "And so, it is with great confidence that I declare my intention to seek a partner among the lovely daughters of this household."

Mrs. Bennet's face lit up with delight, her earlier reservations about Mr. Collins all but forgotten in the face of this unexpected turn of events. "Oh, Mr. Collins, how wonderful! To think that one of my dear girls might be fortunate enough to become your wife and secure the future of Longbourn!"

Elizabeth suppressed a shudder, horrified at the prospect of marrying such a man for the sake of her family's estate.

Lydia, however, seemed more interested in the potential benefits of the arrangement for herself. "Surely, if we are to be related by marriage, I'll have the chance to mingle with all the dashing officers that Lady Catherine's wealth and connections will attract!"

Amidst the flurry of reactions, Mr. Collins continued after a disapproving glance at Lydia, his expression solemn. "Of course, I must ensure that I choose the most deserving and virtuous young lady. I shall make it my mission to observe and engage each of you during my stay, to discern which among you would make the most suitable match."

∽

THAT NIGHT, as the sisters retired to their shared bedroom, Jane and Elizabeth couldn't help but discuss the startling events of the day. The soft glow of the candlelight cast a warm, golden hue over the room.

"Oh, Lizzy," Jane began with a sigh, her expressive eyes filled with concern, "can you believe Mr. Collins' announcement? I can hardly fathom how our lives have become entwined with his in such a manner."

Reclining against a pile of embroidered pillows, Elizabeth replied with a wry smile, "Indeed, it seems that fate has conspired to introduce us to one of the most absurd characters ever to grace our humble abode."

Jane, ever the gentle soul, hesitated before responding. "I do not wish to judge him too harshly, Lizzy. After all, he is family, and it would be unkind to mock him solely for his peculiarities."

"But, Jane," Elizabeth countered, her voice tinged with amusement, "surely you cannot deny that his intentions are rather...extraordinary. To declare his pursuit of one of us so openly, as if we were prizes to be won!"

Jane bit her lip, a faint blush rising to her cheeks. "Yes, I admit it is rather forward of him. But perhaps he is simply eager to fulfill his duty and secure the future of Longbourn for our family."

Elizabeth regarded her sister thoughtfully, the flickering candlelight casting shadows that danced across her intelligent features. "You may be right, and yet, I cannot help but wonder which of us he will ultimately choose. His criteria for a suitable wife seem to be as perplexing as the man himself. Do you think he might choose you, Jane?" Elizabeth asked, her eyes full of concern for her beloved sister. "You are, after all, the eldest and most beautiful of us."

Jane blushed at the compliment but shook her head modestly. "I am not certain, Lizzy. While I would be honored to help secure Longbourn for our family, I must admit that the thought of marrying Mr. Collins is... daunting."

"What about Mary?" Elizabeth mused, a mischievous smile playing on her lips. "Her solemn demeanor and devotion to her studies might appeal to a clergyman such as Mr. Collins."

Jane giggled softly, covering her mouth with her hand to stifle the sound. "Oh, Lizzy, you know as well as I do that Mary would relish the opportunity to engage in such discussions. But can you truly imagine her married to Mr. Collins?"

Elizabeth pursed her lips, considering the unlikely pairing. "It would certainly be...interesting," she admitted. "But in all honesty, I believe even Mary might find herself overwhelmed by his incessant fawning over Lady Catherine de Bourgh."

THE NEXT DAY, the Bennet household was thrown into a mild state of chaos as Mr. Collins devoted himself to evaluating the sisters. He subjected them to a barrage of questions, ranging from their opinions on household management to their proficiency in the genteel arts.

Mrs. Bennet, ever eager to see one of her daughters wed to their prospective benefactor, fervently urged the sisters to display their accomplishments and virtues. However, Elizabeth's sharp wit and disdain for Mr. Collins' pompous demeanor made it increasingly challenging for her to participate in this charade.

Thankfully, Charlotte Lucas paid a visit to Longbourn to discuss the upcoming Netherfield ball, providing a brief reprieve from Mr. Collins. As the two friends chatted animatedly about their plans and expectations for the event, they were interrupted by Mr. Collins entering the room with an air of self-importance.

"Ah, Charlotte," Elizabeth said, gesturing towards their visitor with a flourish, "allow me to introduce you to our cousin, Mr. Collins."

"Mr. Collins, it is a pleasure to make your acquaintance," Charlotte replied, her voice honeyed with politeness.

"Ah, Miss Lucas, the pleasure is entirely mine, I assure you. It is always an honor to meet the esteemed friends of my dear cousins." Mr. Collins bowed deeply, his face glowing with satisfaction.

Charlotte could not help but raise an eyebrow at his peculiar demeanor, though she hid her amusement well. "Thank you."

As Elizabeth tried to steer the conversation back to their previous discussion about the Netherfield ball, Mr. Collins interrupted once again, clearly determined to monopolize her attention.

"Ah, yes, the upcoming ball! I have no doubt that it will be a splendid affair," he exclaimed, clasping his hands together in excitement. "I must admit, I am greatly looking forward to witnessing the elegant dance steps and charming conversation of the ladies present."

Elizabeth cast a pleading glance at Charlotte, who quickly stepped in to rescue her friend from Mr. Collins' relentless attention. "Indeed, Mr. Collins, we were just discussing our hopes for the ball. I, for one, am eager to see the latest fashions on display and enjoy the lively music."

Mr. Collins, temporarily diverted by Charlotte's contribution, nodded vigorously. "Ah, yes, Miss Lucas, that is an excellent point. Lady Catherine herself has often spoken of the importance of good taste and refinement in such events." Turning back to Elizabeth, he gushed, his eyes wide with admiration, "I must say that your wit and intelligence are truly unparalleled among the fairer sex. Indeed, Lady Catherine has often lamented the lack of such qualities in today's young ladies."

Elizabeth, trying her best to maintain her composure, replied with a strained smile. "You are too kind, Mr. Collins. However, I am certain there are many accomplished young women who possess both wit and intelligence."

Unperturbed by her modesty, Mr. Collins continued to sing her praises. "Indeed, Miss Elizabeth, your humility only serves to further endear you to me. I find myself irresistibly drawn to your presence, like a moth to a flame."

Elizabeth's cheeks flushed with embarrassment as she sought to extricate herself from the situation and unwelcome knowledge that she was Mr. Collins' intended bride.

―

THE DAY of the Netherfield Ball had arrived. Elizabeth found herself increasingly preoccupied with whether Mr. Wickham would attend the event, what would occur between the two men, and how she would keep her younger sisters away from the officer.

When the Bennet family arrived at Netherfield Park, the grandeur of the ballroom momentarily took Elizabeth's breath away. As Elizabeth scanned the room and realized Mr. Wickham was not present, a sense of relief washed over her. She was glad for his absence, knowing that the young ladies, including her own sisters, would be safe from any potential harm he could cause.

She soon spotted Charlotte among the guests, resplendent in her carefully chosen attire.

"Charlotte, you look lovely tonight," Elizabeth said with a smile.

"Thank you, Lizzy. And you are as radiant as ever," Charlotte replied, returning the compliment.

As they chatted about the latest gossip and admired the opulent decorations, Elizabeth took solace in the fact that her sisters could enjoy themselves without the threat of Mr. Wickham's influence. Though she remained vigilant, she felt more at ease knowing that the elusive officer was absent from the event.

Their discussion, however, was cut short when Mr. Collins approached, bowing low. "Miss Elizabeth, might I have the honor of requesting the first two dances with you this evening?"

Elizabeth hesitated for just a moment before answering Mr. Collins, her eyes flicking to Charlotte for support. "Of course, Mr. Collins," she replied with a polite smile, masking her reluctance to accept his invitation.

As Mr. Collins walked away to secure his place on the dance floor, Elizabeth turned back to Charlotte with a resigned sigh. "Well, that is two dances spoken for, whether I am looking forward to them or not."

Charlotte chuckled softly, placing a comforting hand on her friend's arm. "Fear not, Lizzy. You are more than capable of enduring a few dances with your esteemed cousin."

Elizabeth smiled at Charlotte's attempt to find a silver lining. "You're right, Charlotte. And who knows? Perhaps Mr. Collins will surprise us all with his dancing prowess."

The two friends shared a knowing look and a muffled giggle. But too soon, Mr. Collins returned and led Elizabeth onto the dance floor with an exaggerated flourish. As they took their places, Elizabeth couldn't help but notice Mr. Darcy standing off to the side, his dark eyes focused intently on her.

To Elizabeth's chagrin, Mr. Collins proceeded to dance in the wrong direction, causing a flurry of confusion amongst the other dancers. Elizabeth's face flushed with embarrassment as she attempted to guide the hapless Mr. Collins back on track.

To her further mortification, she caught Mr. Darcy watching the spectacle with a small, amused smile playing at the corners of his lips.

The dances were over, and having survived the awkward dance with Mr. Collins. Elizabeth sought respite near the refreshment table, her eyes scanning the crowd for familiar faces. To her dismay, Mr. Collins reappeared, seemingly determined to monopolize her attention for the evening.

As Mr. Collins launched into yet another tedious anecdote about Lady Catherine de Bourgh, Elizabeth found herself longing for an escape. "Mr. Collins," she began innocently, "I was wondering if you happened to know a Colonel Fitzwilliam?"

Mr. Collins puffed up with pride at the mention of the man. "Indeed, Miss Elizabeth! Col. Fitzwilliam is the nephew of my esteemed patroness, the Lady Catherine de Bourgh."

Curiosity piqued, Elizabeth pressed further. "Has he ever visited Rosings Park during your time there?"

"Yes, yes, he has graced us with his presence on occasion," Mr. Collins replied, clearly pleased by the direction of their conversation.

Taking a calculated risk, "What can you tell me of Georgiana Darcy? Does she visit Rosings Park often?"

Mr. Collins hesitated for a moment before responding, "Miss Darcy has not visited for some time now, I believe."

Elizabeth ventured another question, her tone casual yet probing. "Is Mr. Darcy her sole guardian?"

To her surprise, Mr. Collins corrected her assumption. "No, my dear cousin. Col. Fitzwilliam shares guardianship of the young lady with Mr. Darcy."

"And does Miss Darcy currently have a governess?" Elizabeth asked.

Mr. Collins knit his brow pensively. "To the best of my knowledge, Miss Darcy currently finds herself without a governess. There was an unfortunate incident involving the prior instructor, which necessitated her removal. I remember both Colonel Fitzwilliam and Mr. Darcy being quite agitated over the affair, though the particulars elude me."

As their tête-à-tête reached its conclusion, Elizabeth felt a surge of triumph wash over her. Mr. Collins' disclosures all but corroborated Mr. Darcy's narrative concerning Mr. Wickham.

While Elizabeth mulled over these revelations, she could not help but observe Lydia and Kitty cavorting about the ballroom, trailed by a retinue of uniformed officers. The two youngest Bennet sisters seemed to revel in the attention, exchanging secretive whispers as they flitted from one gathering to the next.

Under normal circumstances, Elizabeth would maintain vigilant supervision over her impulsive siblings; however, she found herself curiously unperturbed in light of Mr. Wickham's conspicuous absence.

As the evening progressed, Elizabeth became increasingly beleaguered by the persistent attentions of Mr. Collins. Desperate for respite, she scanned the room for sanctuary, only to find herself ensnared by Mr. Darcy's penetrating gaze.

To her amazement, he advanced towards her. "Miss Elizabeth," he intoned, his voice deep and enticing, "may I have the honor of this dance?"

She hesitated briefly, then with a demure, almost coquettish smile, she acquiesced to his request, placing her hand in his as they joined the other couples on the parquet floor.

Gracefully, Elizabeth and Mr. Darcy swept across the dance floor, their movements impeccably synchronized, their bodies drawing nearer than custom would dictate, igniting a frisson of excitement between them.

Seizing the opportunity for discourse, Elizabeth's voice quivered faintly, betraying her burgeoning desire. "Mr. Darcy, I must express my gratitude for your candor regarding Mr. Wickham's true disposition."

Mr. Darcy inclined his head slightly, his eyes smoldering and intense as they held her captive. "You are quite welcome, Miss Elizabeth. It was my obligation to ensure that you were apprised of the facts."

Elizabeth persisted, her heart pounding fiercely, "Your cousin appears to be a gentleman of great integrity and discretion."

A subtle, suggestive smile graced Mr. Darcy's lips as he responded, "Indeed, he is. I place implicit trust in his judgment."

A crackling undercurrent surged between them as they danced, intensifying their smoldering gazes and lingering caresses. Their eyes locked, conveying a longing neither had anticipated. The heat of Mr. Darcy's hand seared through the delicate fabric of Elizabeth's glove, kindling an inferno within that she struggled to suppress.

With every step, twirl, and brush of their hands, the heat between Elizabeth and Mr. Darcy grew more palpable, leaving them both breathless and craving something that propriety forbade them to acknowledge.

As the final strains of the melody dissolved into silence, the pair reluctantly disengaged from one another.

As Elizabeth approached the refreshment table and sipped a glass of punch, Caroline Bingley materialized at her side, her countenance a mask of thinly veiled envy.

"Well," she drawled, appraising Elizabeth with scarcely concealed scorn, "it seems Mr. Darcy has debased himself this evening. One would expect a gentleman of his stature to select a more... fitting partner."

Summoning her inimitable wit and grace, Elizabeth retorted icily, "On the contrary, Miss Bingley, it occasionally requires a truly discerning eye to recognize hidden virtues."

With that, she bestowed upon Caroline Bingley a curt nod and elegantly rejoined her companions.

As the ball continued, Elizabeth found herself both relieved and astonished by Lydia's uncharacteristically circumspect behavior, particularly when compared to her earlier antics. Although her youngest sister still flitted about with palpable enthusiasm, she seemed to eschew any flirtatious dalliances with the officers that might potentially provoke a scandal.

Contemplating the alteration in Lydia's demeanor, Elizabeth deduced that their father must have intervened, imparting a profound effect on her impulsive sibling.

Amidst the swirling kaleidoscope of colors and laughter, Elizabeth cast furtive glances at Mr. Darcy from across the room, her heart skipping a beat whenever their eyes met. The sparking charge between them had only intensified since their dance.

CHAPTER 9

As their carriage swept away from Netherfield, the Bennet family was excited and delighted, each member eagerly recounting the evening's events. The splendid ball had been a whirlwind of dance, laughter, and intrigue that would be the talk of the town for weeks to come.

Upon returning home to Longbourn, Elizabeth sought out her father in his sanctuary – the study where he often retreated to escape the clamor of the household. She found him ensconced in his favorite armchair, a book perched precariously on his knee as he savored the rare peace and quiet.

"Papa," she began, her eyes sparkling with curiosity, "whatever did you say to Lydia? She was positively demure during the second half of the ball."

Mr. Bennet peered at his daughter over the rims of his spectacles, a bemused expression playing across his face. "My dear Lizzy, I assure you that I did not utter a single syllable to Lydia regarding her deportment."

Elizabeth raised an eyebrow in surprise, her mind awash with speculation. "You did not speak to her?"

"No, Elizabeth," Mr. Bennet replied, chuckling at her astonishment. "It seems that young Lydia has managed to temper her exuberance all on her own."

With this perplexing revelation swirling in her thoughts, Elizabeth bid her father goodnight. She glided up the stairs to the chamber she shared with Jane. The room was bathed in the soft glow of candlelight, casting flickering shadows on the walls as the sisters prepared for bed.

Jane's eyes sparkled with a joy that only love-struck hearts can muster. "Oh, Lizzy," she sighed dreamily, her voice melodious, "Mr. Bingley was the epitome of charm and attentiveness tonight."

Elizabeth couldn't help but smile at her sister's bliss, momentarily setting aside her concerns about Lydia's mysterious transformation. "Dearest Jane, it appears that Mr. Bingley is quite smitten with you - and who could blame him?"

As the sisters continued their conversation, their laughter and whispers of newfound romance filled the room, weaving a tapestry of shared memories and secrets that would be cherished for years to come. The Netherfield Ball had been a night of enchantment, intrigue, and unexpected discoveries, leaving an indelible mark on the hearts and minds of all who attended.

~

THE FOLLOWING DAY, Elizabeth awoke to the cacophonous sound of Mrs. Bennet's shrill shrieks echoing through the hallway like a discordant symphony. Blinking away the remnants of sleep, she rose from her bed. She ventured out of her room in her delicate lace-trimmed nightgown, curiosity piqued and heart pounding with trepidation.

In the dimly lit hallway, a scene of pandemonium greeted her – Mrs. Bennet wailing like a banshee, her face streaked with tears; Kitty huddled in a corner, sporting an expression of abject shame; and Mr. Bennet pacing back and forth, his jaw clenched and eyes smoldering with barely contained fury.

As he caught sight of Elizabeth, his face a veritable thundercloud, he stopped abruptly. He exclaimed, "I should have heeded your warnings, Lizzy!"

Her pulse quickened as she asked, the words catching in her throat, "What has happened?" The tension in the air was palpable, and she braced herself for the revelation that would surely shatter their world.

With a trembling voice, Mrs. Bennet interjected, her hands fluttering like distressed birds, "Lydia has eloped with that scoundrel, Mr. Wickham!" The words sent a chill down Elizabeth's spine, her blood turning cold with dread.

Kitty clutched a hastily scrawled note in her shaking hand, which Lydia had left behind.

Elizabeth read the careless words, disbelief and anger rising within her. "How thoughtless and reckless Lydia has been!" She muttered under her breath. Turning to Kitty, she demanded, "How was this even planned? Wickham wasn't at the ball last night."

Kitty hesitated, then whispered, "Lydia received a note during the ball from Wickham asking her to meet him at Longbourn."

Elizabeth felt a momentary relief, hoping that Lydia hadn't planned to run away. Still, Kitty dashed that hope as she added, "Lydia's bag is missing, along with her favorite hat and some dresses."

Mrs. Bennet sobbed uncontrollably, "Oh, Mr. Bingley will never offer for Jane now! Our family is ruined!" She wrung her hands in despair, her eyes brimming with tears.

As Elizabeth took in the gravity of the situation, a wave of guilt washed over her. Could she have prevented this disaster if she had spoken more urgently to Lydia about the dangers of associating with Wickham? Glancing up at Mr. Bennet, she realized the blame was not entirely her own, as he had brushed off her concerns.

At that moment, Mr. Collins emerged from his guest room, his customary pomposity momentarily eclipsed by shock. "I cannot stay under this roof any longer!" He declared pompously, gathering his belongings with uncharacteristic haste. "Such scandalous behavior will reflect poorly upon myself and my esteemed patroness, Lady Catherine de Bourgh. I must take my leave at once."

In the midst of the chaos, Mrs. Bennet hurried after the retreating figure of Mr. Collins, her voluminous skirts billowing behind her like a desperate sail. "Please, Mr. Collins, reconsider!" she implored, her voice tight with panic.

Mr. Collins paused momentarily, his brow furrowed in consternation. "Mrs. Bennet, I must consider my position and the reputation of my esteemed patroness, Lady Catherine de Bourgh. It would be most imprudent for me to remain in the midst of such scandal."

As he continued to his room to pack his belongings, Mrs. Bennet's face flushed with indignation. She turned her wrath upon the hapless Kitty. "You foolish girl!" she scolded sharply. "Why did you not inform us immediately about Wickham's note? We might have been able to prevent this disaster!"

Kitty's lip quivered, tears welling up in her eyes as she cried, "It's not my fault, Mama! I didn't run away with him – Lydia did!"

Mr. Bennet intervened with an authoritative tone. "Enough, both of you! There is no sense in tearing each other apart over what has already come to pass. Kitty, you will be grounded until further notice. You shall use this time to reflect upon the importance of discretion and loyalty to one's family."

Kitty sniffled, nodding her acquiescence as she dabbed at her tear-stained cheeks.

Elizabeth couldn't help but wonder what Mr. Darcy would think of the debacle befalling her family. Would he see her in a different light, tainted by association? Would he be glad that she had refused his offer of marriage?

A sudden, disconcerting realization struck Elizabeth – the unexpected missive from Wickham must have been the catalyst for Lydia's uncharacteristic decorum during the second half of the ball. She recalled how she had playfully congratulated Mr. Bennet on the very same improved behavior, blissfully unaware of the impending storm it portended. Elizabeth ruefully shook her head at her own naivete.

Retreating to her shared bedroom to change, she couldn't help but feel a twinge of ironic amusement at the situation. Who would have thought that Wickham's devious machinations would so effectively masquerade as a welcome improvement in Lydia's conduct?

As she changed into her day dress, Elizabeth's thoughts strayed to Mr. Darcy, and she found herself wondering if he would ever look upon her with those smoldering eyes again. The memory of their charged encounters sent a shiver down her spine, even as she acknowledged the seemingly insurmountable obstacles now standing between them.

∾

Mr. Darcy and Mr. Bingley cantered to Longbourn on spirited steeds, their hearts aflutter with a heady mix of nervous excitement and anticipation. Mr. Bingley steeled himself to seize the opportunity and beseech Jane's hand in marriage, his heart nearly bursting at the seams with eagerness. As for Mr. Darcy, he was keen to cast his gaze once more upon the woman whose bewitching allure had haunted his dreams ever since.

No sooner had they dismounted than Mr. Collins burst through the front door, his visage flushed and flustered. Upon recognizing Mr. Darcy, he addressed him with a curious blend of desperation and obsequiousness. "Mr. Darcy, as the nephew of my esteemed patroness Lady Catherine de Bourgh, might I impose upon you for shelter for one night? I cannot remain in this house any longer due to the scandal that has befallen it."

Both Mr. Darcy and Mr. Bingley exchanged worried glances, and a chorus of concern rose from their lips in unison, "What scandal?"

Before Mr. Collins could divulge the sordid details, Elizabeth emerged from within the house, her cheeks flushed and her eyes alight with panic. "Mr. Collins, what are you doing? Please stop and come back inside at once!"

But heedless of Elizabeth's plea, Mr. Collins proceeded to recount the unfortunate events that had transpired within the Bennet household, much to the dismay of Mr. Darcy and Mr. Bingley.

Heart heavy with disappointment and concern, Mr. Bingley reluctantly told Mr. Collins, "Please inform Miss Bennet that I called on her, though I understand if she does not wish to see me at this time."

With that, both gentlemen took their leave, the weight of the revelation hanging leaden between them. As for Mr. Collins, he did not relay Mr. Bingley's message to the Bennets – whether out of spite or sheer forgetfulness remained unclear. Instead, he set off towards Meryton, waddling under the burden of his heavy bags, leaving behind a whirlwind of chaos and heartache.

A deep sense of despair enshrouded Elizabeth. The scandal had not only driven away Mr. Collins but seemed to have dashed any hopes of Jane's happiness with Mr. Bingley. Amidst this turmoil, Elizabeth found herself thinking of Mr. Darcy. She couldn't help but wonder if this could have been prevented had she accepted Mr. Darcy's impulsive offer of marriage at the pond. At least then, their family would have one daughter engaged, ensuring care and security for them all after Mr. Bennet's eventual passing.

A FRANTIC MR. Bennet sought out Colonel Forster. "How did this happen?" he demanded, his voice trembling with anger and desperation. "How did you not know Wickham better?"

Colonel Forster, taken aback by Mr. Bennet's fervor, hesitated before responding. "It is difficult to judge a man's character completely, sir," he said carefully. "But it is also important that young ladies behave properly. As for your concerns, you don't need to go to London. Mr. Darcy has already departed, claiming he had a history with Wickham and should have warned us all."

Stunned by this revelation, Mr. Bennet's thoughts raced back to Elizabeth's warning regarding Wickham, which he had dismissed as mere jealousy on the part of Mr. Darcy. The terrible truth settled even more heavily upon his shoulders.

After returning to Longbourn and stating his intent to hunt down the scoundrel, his youngest daughter, Mrs. Bennet, ever the dramatic creature, wailed as if the world were ending. "Oh, my nerves! Mr. Bennet, you cannot go to London and call Wickham out! You will be shot, and we shall all be ruined!" She lamented, her sobs echoing throughout the house.

Amid the chaos, Jane did her best to maintain a brave front despite the turmoil within her heart. Mr. Bingley had promised to call on her after the ball, yet she had heard nothing. The silence weighed heavily upon her, adding to the cloud of despair that hung over the Bennet household.

CHAPTER 10

A storm of emotions raged within Mr. Darcy as he retreated to his quarters, his thoughts racing and heart pounding with equal measures of concern and determination.

The door swung open, revealing an apprehensive Mr. Bingley standing in the doorway. "Darcy?" he inquired, his voice laced with both sympathy and curiosity. "What are you doing?"

Pausing momentarily from directing his valet in his haphazard packing, Mr. Darcy looked up at his friend, his eyes filled with regret. "Bingley, this is my fault. I should have warned everyone about Wickham. I cannot abide idly by any longer while he wreaks havoc on innocent lives."

Mr. Bingley, although somewhat taken aback by his friend's intensity, nodded in understanding. "How do you plan to find him?"

"I shall start by locating Georgiana's former governess – the one with a previous association with Wickham. She must know something of his whereabouts or at least where he might seek refuge." Mr. Darcy's hands clenched into fists.

Mr. Bingley's eyebrows shot up in surprise. "You mean to go traipsing after Wickham yourself? Darcy, that rogue is dangerous. You cannot gallivant off into the countryside without protection."

Mr. Darcy waved a dismissive hand, not pausing in his packing. "I shall take my pistols and wits, which have always served me well enough."

Mr. Bingley frowned. "At least promise me you'll take some of my men for backup."

"If it will put you at ease," Mr. Darcy agreed. His friend meant well, though Mr. Darcy doubted any number of retainers would deter Wickham if he wished for confrontation. His vendetta was personal. "I mean to leave at once. There is no time to waste."

As Mr. Bingley left, Mr. Darcy's thoughts strayed to Elizabeth and her fine eyes, so recently filled with delight in his company. The memory only fueled his determination. He would hunt down the dastardly Wickham and put an end to his nefarious schemes before the blackguard could irrevocably soil Elizabeth's pristine reputation and extinguish any glimmer of hope Mr. Darcy held of claiming her hand.

With his loyal valet and a handful of armed sentries as his allies, Mr. Darcy embarked upon the dusty road to London. Though Wickham may have vanished into the roiling sea of the city streets, Mr. Darcy possessed sources and means enough for ferreting out a weasel-like him. "On to Newholm lodgings, the consequences be damned!" Mr. Darcy commanded, spurring his mount ahead of his men as the thrill of the chase thrummed through his veins.

∼

FILLED with determination and a sense of responsibility, Mr. Bennet traveled to London to stay with his brother-in-law, Mr. Gardiner. He was at a loss as to what exactly he should do or where to look, but the need to take action was overpowering. The guilt weighed heavily on him for not listening to Elizabeth when she had initially expressed her concerns about Wickham.

Upon arriving at the Gardiners' residence, Mr. Bennet found himself seeking solace in drink, staying up late into the night, attempting to drown his sorrows and clear his thoughts. As he sat in the dimly lit drawing room, a new supper before him, Mr. Bennet brooded over his role in bringing such disgrace upon his family.

"I should have heeded your warnings, Lizzy," he muttered into his glass. "Instead, I allowed my own folly and pride to blind me to the potential danger."

Mr. Gardiner, who had joined him in the room, placed a comforting hand on his brother-in-law's shoulder. "You cannot blame yourself entirely, Thomas," he said gently. "We are all guilty of placing too much trust in appearances, and Wickham has proven himself to be a master at deceiving those around him."

Mr. Bennet sighed heavily, his gaze distant and filled with regret. "And now I must find a way to repair the damage, to restore my family's honor, and secure my daughters' futures."

As the candlelight flickered across the room, casting shadows on the somber faces of both men, they fell into a contemplative silence.

The following day, Mr. Bennet wandered through the streets of London, searching for any clue that might lead him to Wickham and his missing daughter. His days were consumed by this quest, the guilt gnawing at him as he retraced his steps and pondered where he had gone wrong and how he could right the situation.

At night, Mr. Bennet would return to the Gardiners' home, exhausted yet unable to sleep, tormented by thoughts of what might be happening to Lydia and the potential consequences for his family. He would sit by the fading embers in the fireplace, a glass of port in hand, while Mr. Gardiner provided a sympathetic ear, offering advice and reassurance whenever possible.

Exhausted from his internal struggles, Mr. Bennet was still in bed the following morning when Mr. Darcy arrived, eager to speak with Mr. Gardiner.

"Mr. Gardiner," Mr. Darcy began, his voice urgent yet composed, "I have located Wickham, and we must act promptly to arrange a marriage contract between him and your niece."

Stunned by this revelation, Mr. Gardiner wasted no time in agreeing to accompany Mr. Darcy, eager to resolve the situation and secure his family's reputation. As they left the house to work out the terms of the arrangement, Mr. Bennet, having been roused by the commotion, stumbled out of his room, bleary-eyed and disheveled.

"What is happening?" he mumbled groggily, rubbing his eyes as he tried to make sense of the situation.

Mrs. Gardiner, who had overheard the conversation between her husband and Mr. Darcy, quickly filled Mr. Bennet in on the latest developments.

Mr. Bennet sank into a chair, his knees suddenly weak. "Can it be true? Has that scoundrel actually been found and agreed to do right by Lydia?"

Mrs. Gardiner nodded, her eyes glistening with tears of joy and sympathy for her brother's anguish. "Thanks to Mr. Darcy, it seems this whole dreadful business shall be resolved, and the family's good name restored."

"Bless that man. I have misjudged him entirely." he released a shuddering sigh, grasping his sister-in-law's hand.

~

JANE SIGHED, staring listlessly out the window of her bedchamber as yet another day slipped by without a word from Mr. Bingley. His promise to call again dwelt in her thoughts, a sweet torture she could not escape though a sennight had passed since the Netherfield ball.

Below stairs, Elizabeth paced the corridors in agitation, unable to settle her mind. Her concern for Jane's wounded heart mingled with fears for Lydia's reputation and their family's good name, hovering like a pall over the estate. With Mrs. Bennet confined to her rooms and Mr. Bennet away in London, the duty to maintain order and good sense fell entirely upon her shoulders. It was a burden she felt ill-equipped to bear alone.

A sharp rap at the door heralded the arrival of her aunt, Mrs. Philips, on one of her regular calls to gossip and cluck in sympathy over her sister's poor nerves. Though silly and often vexing, even Aunt Philips' chatter was a welcome distraction today.

Mrs. Philips bustled into the foyer in a flurry of skirts and chatter. "An express letter has just arrived postmarked London! Open it, open it!"

Mrs. Philips thrust the letter into her niece's hands. With trembling fingers, Elizabeth unfolded the missive. She quickly scanned its contents, fearing Lydia had not been found or, worse, that Mr. Bennet had been injured in a duel with Wickham.

Relief flooded her senses, and she sank onto a nearby chair as her legs threatened to give way beneath her. "Can this be true?" she breathed.

"What does it say? Do not keep us in suspense!"

"Lydia has been found and even now is being wed to Mr. Wickham!" Elizabeth cried out.

Mrs. Philips clapped her hands together gleefully. "Is it not splendid? Your sister's reputation is preserved, and your family is saved from ruin! Oh, I must go to your poor mother directly. She will be overjoyed!"

As her aunt hurried upstairs to share the good news, Elizabeth pressed the letter to her chest, overcome with gratitude. They were saved. Lydia was found and to be respectably wed. She let out a shaky laugh, wiping at the tears of joy and worry that spilled onto her cheeks.

The ensuing cries from upstairs could have roused the slumbering dead. "Married? Oh, blessings from above! However, she simply cannot wed in those tattered garments she took with her. Lizzy, you must send a message posthaste and insist they postpone until I select an appropriate trousseau. The fabric in that region will be abominable, and she must consider her position as a new bride!"

Elizabeth shook her head, endearingly exasperated. Trust her mother to rise from potential disgrace, preoccupied with matters of fashion and status.

Clasping the express in her hands, Elizabeth ascended the stairs to Jane's room, tapping gently before entering with a beaming smile. "The most marvelous tidings! Lydia and Wickham have been discovered. They are currently exchanging vows, ensuring our family's reputation remains unblemished."

Jane's responding grin was radiant as the sisters embraced, their worries and sorrows dissipating in a deluge of relief and laughter. Jane held Elizabeth close, overwhelmed with joy at the assurance of Lydia's reputation and future happiness.

"Dearest Lizzy, what splendid news! I am profoundly grateful that Lydia's predicament has been resolved, and I shall pray her marriage is filled with bliss." Although her own tender hopes had been severely tested recently, Jane's kind heart could not deny her sister this celebratory moment.

Elizabeth regarded her sister with affectionate vexation. Even now, Jane prioritized others' well-being before her own. "Fear not; I have not forgotten your own recent melancholy. With the cloud of scandal dispelled and Lydia's good name restored, I am confident Mr. Bingley will pay you a visit ere long."

Jane gazed wistfully out the window, her lips curving into a poignant smile. "While I appreciate your attempts to lift my spirits, I have come to terms with the fact that Mr. Bingley's affections have strayed. His kindness shall forever remain in my memory, a glimmer of joy to warm my heart on colder days."

"You must not forsake hope so readily," Elizabeth urged, taking her sister's hands. "Mr. Bingley esteemed you above all others. I am sure an explanation for his absence will soon be revealed, and when it is, he will hasten back to your side."

Jane shook her head, maintaining her grace and poise even amidst sorrow. Elizabeth observed her sister with a mix of love, frustration, and admiration. Jane's compassion was boundless; her ability to wish joy and fulfillment upon others, even at her own expense, set her apart from most in their social circle.

"Now we must go downstairs before Mama commences planning an extravagant ball to commemorate Lydia's wedding," Elizabeth declared, feigning cheerfulness as she linked her arm through Jane's.

∽

Lydia pouted as the carriage jostled over the cobblestone lane toward the modest village church. "This is far from the wedding of my dreams. Mama and my sisters should be here, and it ought to have taken place at the church in Meryton, surrounded by my friends."

Mr. Bennet sighed, his head throbbing from a sleepless night spent worrying about scandalous whispers behind fluttering fans and sly remarks from neighbors. "You should count yourself fortunate there is even a wedding, you silly girl, after the grief you have caused this family."

Lydia sniffed. "It is all so dreary and dull. At least, my dear Wickham will be there to brighten the occasion."

Mr. Gardiner shook his head in disbelief at his niece's obstinate refusal to comprehend the magnitude of her reckless actions. By some miracle, they had managed to gather enough of Wickham's debts to persuade the scoundrel into this rushed ceremony, saving the family from utter ruin. And yet, the young woman remained fixated on her own appearance in the latest French lace and silks.

The carriage halted before the weathered doors of the church as two raggedy boys scrambled to assist the ladies in alighting. Within, Mr. Wickham waited at the altar, impatience carved into the harsh lines of his face until the sight of his bride rekindled a practiced charm.

Lydia floated down the aisle, blissfully ignorant of her new husband's rather mercenary motivations for agreeing to matrimony. As the vicar droned through the ceremony, Mr. Darcy stood absorbed in contemplation of what other trials they might uncover regarding Wickham's misdeeds within the militia.

Finally, the closing benediction was pronounced, and the newlywed Wickhams turned to greet their guests. Lydia's lively chatter reverberated throughout the chamber, an effusive torrent of foolishness and exclamations over being the first of her sisters to marry. Mr. Bennet looked on, torn between relief at his daughter's redemption and apprehension about what other antics her unchecked frivolity might incite from the charming rogue she had chosen as her lifelong partner.

CHAPTER 11

Mr. Bennet heaved a weary sigh as the carriage turned down the lane toward Longbourn, his head pounding from the tumult of Lydia's hurried wedding. Although her reputation was saved, he harbored no illusions about the character of the man she had taken as her husband. She was fortunate there had been a wedding at all.

As the carriage rolled to a stop before the house, Mrs. Bennet burst out the door in a flurry of nerves and chatter. "Are the newlyweds behind you? How splendid Mr. Wickham must have looked in his uniform! And my dear Lydia, what a vision she must have made in her bridal gown."

Jane and Elizabeth exchanged knowing glances, both relieved that the situation had been resolved but acutely aware of the lingering stigma attached to their sister's actions.

Mr. Bennet alighted from the carriage, leaning heavily upon his walking stick. "Your new son has gone to take up his new orders and shall bring your daughter here directly."

"How very fine to have an officer in the family," Mrs. Bennet preened as they walked inside. "And all thanks to you, my dear —"

"Do not thank me," Mr. Bennet said wearily. "Thank Mr. Darcy and your brother Gardiner. They did all the work in uncovering Wickham's debts and convincing the scoundrel to do right by Lydia."

Elizabeth's head shot up in surprise from where she was arranging flowers in the foyer. "Mr. Darcy was involved in arranging the wedding?"

Mr. Bennet removed his hat and gloves with a sigh. "Aye, it seems I owe the man an apology for speaking ill of him. Without his interference and your uncle's resources, Lydia's reputation and our family's good name would have been in tatters."

Elizabeth stared in shock, her mind working to understand why Mr. Darcy would go to such lengths to aid a family he disdained and a man he openly reviled.

"Forgive me, Lizzy, for not heeding your warnings about Wickham's character," Mr. Bennet said heavily. "My foolish blindness has brought no end of trouble."

"All is resolved now, Papa," Elizabeth replied gently. "Let us be grateful that our family's preservation and peace are restored once more."

Still, her thoughts lingered on the puzzle Mr. Darcy presented. Tears glistened in Elizabeth's eyes as her heart swelled with gratitude towards Mr. Darcy. Despite everything that had transpired between them, he had chosen to step in and save her family from ruin. The depth of his actions only served to intensify the complicated emotions she felt for him.

Mrs. Bennet's excited shrieks heralded the approach of Lydia and her new husband, putting an end to further discussion. As Lydia swept into the foyer in a flourish of lace and laughter, chattering gaily about her wedding, Elizabeth exchanged a glance with her father. While the future remained uncertain, for good or ill, Mr. Wickham was now irrevocably tied to their family. She could only hope Lydia might gain wisdom in time.

"Oh, Mama, such a splendid wedding it was!" Lydia exclaimed, embracing her mother enthusiastically. "The church was filled to the brim, and all of society turned out to congratulate us."

Elizabeth frowned. Had Lydia already forgotten the hastily arranged ceremony in the small church?

"And my dear Mr. Wickham was the most handsome groom," Lydia said, gazing up at her new husband in adoration. "Everyone remarked on what a charming couple we made."

"I am delighted the day met with your satisfaction, Mrs. Wickham," Mr. Bennet said dryly. He turned a stern eye to his new son-in-law. "No thanks to you for the grief you have caused this family. I trust you shall endeavor to do right by my daughter and prevent future scandal."

Mr. Wickham bowed, the picture of remorse, though his eyes glinted with resentment at the reprimand. "You have my word, sir. I shall devote myself entirely to ensuring my new bride's happiness and good name."

Lydia pouted prettily, clinging to her husband's arm. "Do not be cross with my dear Wickham, Papa. We are married now, so all is forgiven."

Elizabeth gazed at her sister with a mixture of exasperation and pity. Lydia had learned nothing from her misadventures and placed herself entirely under the power and charm of Mr. Wickham. She could only hope his devotion and good behavior would last beyond the heady days of newlywed bliss.

That afternoon, Elizabeth and her sisters left Longbourn for a walk in the countryside. As they strolled down the lane, Mr. Wickham rode past on horseback, tipping his hat and flashing a charming smile at Lydia, leaving her giggling and blushing.

When he had disappeared from view, Elizabeth turned to her sister. "Lydia, I was surprised to hear Mr. Darcy was involved in arranging your wedding."

Lydia shrugged. "I did not inquire into the particulars. I was simply grateful dear Wickham came to his senses at last."

Elizabeth shook her head in frustration. "Do you not wonder how Mr. Darcy came to be aiding a man he despises? The makings of your match must have been quite a trial if it required his interference."

"Mr. Darcy's actions are of no consequence to me," Lydia said airily. "Now that Wickham and I are wed, the past troubles are behind us."

Jane gazed at Lydia in concern. "Still, one must wonder what debts or scandals Mr. Darcy uncovered to convince Mr. Wickham into matrimony. Do you not worry he may revert to his old ways?"

Lydia's eyes flashed. "Not another word against my dear Wickham! He has promised to amend his ways, and I trust him utterly. Must you all cast shadows over my happiness with your doubts and reproaches?"

Elizabeth sighed in frustration as Lydia stomped off down the lane in a fit of pique. Any wisdom or prudence their sister may have gained would come too late. She had bound herself to Mr. Wickham for life, willfully ignoring his failings and the circumstances that had very nearly led to her ruin.

Jane slipped her arm gently through Elizabeth's as they strolled back to Longbourn. "Do not despair over much for Lydia's sake. Though her marriage began in scandal, she is young and light of heart. Perhaps time and affection will transform Mr. Wickham into the husband she deserves."

Elizabeth gazed at her sister in mute appeal. Jane's propensity to see the best in all and hope for improbable outcomes was at once her most endearing and vexing trait. While Lydia basked in wedded bliss and saw only the charm in her new husband, Elizabeth harbored grave doubts about the man who had so nearly brought their family low without a shred of conscience.

∽

THE FOLLOWING DAY, the Bennet family gathered in the drive to bid farewell to the Wickhams as they prepared to depart for his new commission in the North. Lydia held her hand out the carriage window, displaying her wedding ring prominently, eager to garner attention as they rode through Meryton.

Mrs. Bennet dabbed at her eyes with a handkerchief, bereft at the thought of her favorite daughter moving so far away. "It is not to be borne that you must travel so very far north! If only Colonel Forster had not sent you to such a remote outpost, I would not lose my dear Lydia."

Mr. Bennet shook his head at his wife's usual ridiculous logic. Still, he remained uncharacteristically solemn as he gazed at the carriage. For all Lydia's silly chatter and willful ignorance of what her elopement had nearly cost them, she was still his daughter. He could not deny a pang of sadness to see her going forth into the uncertain future that awaited Mrs. Wickham.

Kitty clung to her handkerchief, sobbing at the imminent loss of her sister and confidante. "I shall miss you desperately, Lydia! No one shall understand me as you always have."

Lydia gazed upon her sister through the carriage window. "There, there, Kitty. Do not weep! Though we may be parted for a time, we shall meet again, and I shall regale you with letters brimming with tales from the North to cheer you."

Elizabeth tenderly placed a comforting hand on Kitty's shoulder while casting a furtive glance at the husband who had won her sister's hand at no small cost. Mr. Wickham grinned and waved, the charming scoundrel to the last, though his eyes betrayed hints of restlessness at being thus tethered to the Bennets' country life. She harbored more than a few doubts about his ability to remain faithful and provide for Lydia's happiness. However, she hoped to be proven wrong for her sister's sake.

As the carriage rolled away down the lane, bearing Lydia to her new life, an unsettling mix of sadness, apprehension, and relief descended over those left behind. The house would feel Lydia's absence and noisy vivacity most keenly. However, Elizabeth suspected her father, in particular, would find repose in the quieter days to come.

Still, Lydia was her sister, for better and worse, and the miles that would soon separate them left Elizabeth with a certain melancholy. She gazed at the empty lane as the carriage vanished from view.

The house settled into silence as the family slowly retreated indoors, each absorbed in their own thoughts. Elizabeth was uncertain what the coming days might hold. Mr. Bingley had still not called on Jane since Lydia's wedding. Nor had she seen or heard of Mr. Darcy other than what Lydia had disclosed. Why had he taken so much upon himself for their family that he disliked so? The uncertainty of what was to come unsettled her, and she found the walls of Longbourn stifling.

Slipping out the back door, Elizabeth made her way to the woods where she had always found solace. The day was overcast but not unbearably hot, so she ambled down to the pond, idly picking up stones and attempting to skip them across the glassy surface.

After several failed attempts, a familiar voice spoke behind her. "You need to select a flatter stone and flick your wrist as you throw."

Elizabeth shrieked in surprise, stumbling on the bank and tumbling into the pond with an enormous splash. She stood in the water, soaked to the skin, to find Mr. Darcy gazing at her in alarm from the shore.

"Good heavens, Miss Elizabeth, are you quite well?"

"I am fine, though rather damp at the moment, thanks to you."

"You must come out directly and change into dry clothes." His stern voice was laced with concern as he took in her bedraggled state.

Elizabeth gazed up at him in vexation. "And whose fault is it that I find myself in this condition?"

The corners of Mr. Darcy's mouth twitched, though his smile faded as he took in her soaked gown. "I must beg your pardon, Miss Elizabeth. I had not intended to startle you into the pond."

Elizabeth scowled in reply.

Mr. Darcy gazed at her with tender concern, his smile vanishing. "Come, let me escort you home before you fall ill." He offered his arm to help her out of the pond, all hints of teasing gone.

Elizabeth gazed up at him in surprise at the earnest worry in his voice. Though irritated with him for causing her abrupt plunge into the pond, she could not remain angry in the face of his evident care for her wellbeing. Her vexation melted away, replaced by a fluttering in her breast she did not dare examine too closely.

"I heard you were in London at Lydia's wedding," Elizabeth said. "Thank you for your interference on her behalf. My family is deeply indebted to you."

Mr. Darcy gazed down at her, his expression inscrutable. "I did not do it for your family. I did it for you."

Elizabeth stared at him in shock, uncertain how to reply. Mr. Darcy returned her gaze with an intensity that left her breathless. She glanced down at her sodden gown. "It would not be appropriate for me to continue our conversation in this state. My dress..."

"I have seen you in a wet dress before, Miss Elizabeth," Mr. Darcy replied, one brow arched. At her indignant look, he sighed and secured his horse's reins to a nearby tree.

Elizabeth's eyes widened in alarm as he began removing his coat, waistcoat, and cravat. "Mr. Darcy! Whatever are you doing?"

"I am going to join you." He kicked off his boots, walking into the pond in only his shirt and breeches. Elizabeth sputtered in protest, but he held up a hand. "I wished to speak with you, and you refuse to emerge from the pond. Desperate times call for desperate measures."

Elizabeth could only gaze at him in mute shock, torn between laughter at the absurdity of the situation and mortification at the impropriety as Mr. Darcy waded over to join her. "This is highly irregular, sir!"

"So is plunging into ponds fully clothed," he replied, the corner of his mouth twitching. He gazed down at Elizabeth with an earnestness that stole her breath. "I have struggled these many weeks to find the words, and I can resist no longer. You have bewitched me, body and soul, Miss Elizabeth. From the first moment of our acquaintance, you have intrigued and infuriated me by turns. I think of you constantly and dream of the day when I might call you my own."

Elizabeth stared up at him, stunned to silence. She had never imagined his interference on Lydia's behalf was motivated by feelings for her rather than duty. His confession left her reeling with questions and warring emotions. She knew not how to reply.

Mr. Darcy gazed at her in tender concern, uncertain how his heartfelt words had been received. "I fear I have distressed you. Such was not my intent." He sighed and turned to climb from the pond. "Forgive me. I should not have imposed upon you in your current state."

Elizabeth reached out and caught his hand before he could leave the water. "No, do not leave." She searched his face, her heart swelling. "You have long been in my thoughts as well, though I did not dare hope my feelings might be returned."

Joy suffused Mr. Darcy's features as the meaning of her words registered. He pulled her into his arms and kissed her thoroughly, no longer caring they were standing ankle-deep in a pond. Elizabeth clung to him, returning his ardor with a warmth that left them both breathless.

When they finally broke apart, chests heaving and pulses racing, they gazed at each other in tender bemusement to find they were now covered in mud and sopping wet. Laughter bubbled up at the absurdity of the situation, easing the last vestiges of uncertainty.

Mr. Darcy climbed out of the pond and lifted Elizabeth onto his horse, mud and all, before swinging up behind her. "You are a sight, Miss Elizabeth," he said, chuckling.

"As are you, sir," she replied archly, though she could not stop smiling.

Mr. Darcy and Elizabeth, still giggling from the spectacle they made, rode towards Longbourn on his horse. Darcy sat behind Elizabeth, one arm wrapped securely around her waist. His other hand held the reins, guiding the horse at a leisurely canter down the lane.

Elizabeth's cheeks were flushed, though from their passionate kiss or their compromising position, she knew not which. Her heart swelled near to bursting with felicity.

As they neared the house, they could hear the excitement emanating from inside while another horse was tethered to the hitching post.

CHAPTER 12

*E*lizabeth's curiosity was piqued by the commotion, and she inquired of Mr. Darcy, "Who do you suppose is visiting? I see another horse tethered nearby, and quite a stir emanates from within."

Mr. Darcy's lips curved into a knowing smile as he replied, "Bingley had planned to call on Jane today. It seems our arrival might coincide with his."

A look of happiness and hope flitted across Elizabeth's face as she considered the possibility that Mr. Bingley might be offering for her dearest sister, Jane. "I do hope it means good news for Jane," she murmured softly.

With laughter still bubbling between them, the couple dismounted the horse. Elizabeth gasped as Mr. Darcy swung her down, her drenched skirts clinging to her legs. Catching their disheveled, mud-spattered reflections in the windows of Longbourn, she burst into laughter once more.

Mr. Darcy chuckled, pulling Elizabeth close for another lingering kiss. "Much as I long to continue where we left off, I fear we have already caused enough scandal for one day," he murmured with a rueful smile.

Elizabeth sighed, leaning into his embrace. "Must we go inside? I am loath to face my mother in this state."

"Nor do I wish to speak to your father coated in mud," Mr. Darcy replied, his eyes alight with mischief. "Though the look on Mrs. Bennet's face upon seeing us thus might almost be worth it."

As they shared a knowing grin, a servant emerged from the front door and started in surprise at the sight of them. Her eyes grew round as saucers, taking in their disheveled and muddy appearances.

"Hill, whatever is the matter?" Elizabeth asked while giggling.

Before she could say anything, Mrs. Bennet's shrill voice called from within the house. "Hill! Why are you standing in the doorway when you were supposed to fetch Lizzy?"

The servant hastily replied, "Mrs. Bennet, Miss Elizabeth, and Mr. Darcy have just arrived. They are both covered in mud and quite wet, ma'am."

At this news, Mrs. Bennet, Jane, and her newly betrothed Mr. Bingley hurried outside to see the spectacle for themselves. Jane rushed to Elizabeth, embracing her carefully despite her sister's sodden clothes.

"Oh, Lizzy! I am so happy! It is too much. He loves me, Lizzy, and we are engaged!" Jane exclaimed, her eyes shining with happiness.

"Of course he does. I am so happy for you, dear sister," Elizabeth replied, tears of happiness pricking at her eyes.

Mrs. Bennet, however, was not content to let the matter of her second eldest daughter's disheveled appearance rest. "Lizzy, what on earth has happened to you? And why are you and Mr. Darcy both drenched and besmirched with mud?"

Elizabeth replied with a sheepish smile that failed to mask her flushed cheeks, "I was attempting to skip stones across the pond when Mr. Darcy unexpectedly appeared behind me, and I inadvertently lost my footing and fell in."

At that moment, Mr. Bennet emerged onto the scene, having been alerted to the commotion outside. Angrily surveying his favorite daughter's state, he asked, "What is the meaning of this? What have you done to my dear Lizzy?"

Elizabeth hastily interjected, striving to placate her father, "Oh, Mr. Darcy merely startled me while I was merrily skipping stones. There was nothing nefarious about it." She blushed as her father scrutinized her and Darcy with unwavering intensity.

Mr. Bennet narrowed his eyes, the lines on his brow deepening. "I will not tolerate another scandal within this family."

Elizabeth protested, her voice strained with anxiety, "Papa!"

Mr. Darcy stepped forward, his posture resolute and demeanor earnest. "Sir, I assure you that my intentions are entirely honorable. In fact, I sought your daughter's agreement for marriage earlier today at the pond."

Mr. Bennet regarded him warily, but there was a glimmer of approval in his eyes.

Overhearing the exchange, Mrs. Bennet could barely contain her elation, exclaiming in delight, "Two daughters engaged in a single day! Such unparalleled happiness!"

In the midst of Mrs. Bennet's exuberant outburst, Kitty and Mary emerged from within Longbourn, curious as to the cause of their mother's excitement. They looked on in surprise as the scene unfolded before them, their eyes wide with astonishment at the sight of Elizabeth and Mr. Darcy standing together, muddy and soaking wet.

"My dear girls," she exclaimed, clapping her hands together, "can you believe our good fortune? First Jane, and now Lizzy! Both engaged to such distinguished gentlemen! Why, we shall be the envy of Meryton! And to think," Mrs. Bennet continued, her voice brimming with pride, "that I have managed to see two of my dear daughters so well settled. Oh, what happy days await us!"

"Mama, please, I must change before catching a cold," Elizabeth insisted.

"Oh yes, of course, run along!" Mrs. Bennet shooed her away distractedly, her mind already whirring with thoughts of guest lists, menus, and linens.

As Elizabeth gratefully retreated into Longbourn, Mr. Darcy took his cue to make his own escape. "Mr. Bennet, I must beg your indulgence. I need to change into more suitable attire before we properly discuss the upcoming nuptials. If you will permit me, I shall return to Netherfield for a brief period and come back shortly."

"Of course, Mr. Darcy," Mr. Bennet replied with an understanding nod. "We shall eagerly await your return."

Mr. Bingley chimed in, "I shall accompany you, Darcy. I cannot wait to share my happy news with my sisters!"

As the gentlemen rode away from Longbourn, Elizabeth hurried inside to change out of their damp garments, her heart swelling with happiness at the joyful events of the day.

Mr. Bingley burst into the drawing room at Netherfield, beaming with delight. His sisters, Caroline and Louisa, glanced up in surprise.

"Such happy news, sisters!" Bingley exclaimed. "I have proposed to Jane Bennet, and she has consented to be my wife!"

Caroline's countenance fell though she attempted a weak smile. "How...splendid, Charles. And what of Mr. Darcy? He rode out with you earlier. I do hope he has come to no harm riding about the countryside in this inclement weather."

"Darcy is quite well," Bingley replied, oblivious to his sister's transparent maneuvering. "In fact, he has an announcement of his own to make, though I shall let him share it in his own time."

At this, Caroline shared a long look with her sister. Just then, Mr. Darcy entered the room, freshly attired in dry clothes, though still uncharacteristically disheveled and with damp hair.

At the sight of him, Caroline fluttered her eyelashes coquettishly. "Mr. Darcy, I am glad to see you have returned safely. You must have had quite an eventful morning. Charles mentioned you needed to change?"

"Indeed. Bingley has apprised you of his happy news?" Mr. Darcy smiled, though his eyes remained distant.

"He has," Caroline replied. "And…he mentioned you have news as well? Is Georgiana coming to visit?"

A small, knowing smile played on Mr. Darcy's lips. "No, my news concerns a matter rather closer to home. Miss Elizabeth Bennet has accepted my proposal of marriage."

Caroline's face paled, and Louisa inhaled sharply, both sisters rendered nearly speechless by the unexpected revelation.

After a moment, Louisa managed to find her voice, attempting a lighthearted tone. "My goodness, Mr. Darcy! It seems Hertfordshire has cast its spell upon not one but two eligible gentlemen."

Mr. Darcy's smile deepened, undeterred by their thinly veiled disapproval. "Indeed, it seems the charm of the Bennet sisters is not to be underestimated."

Caroline, finally recovering herself, chimed in though her voice trembled slightly. "Well, I must say, we never would have anticipated such an outcome when we first arrived at Netherfield. Who could have foreseen our dear brother Charles and yourself being so delightfully beguiled?"

Mr. Darcy inclined his head with a graceful, courtly bow, acutely aware of the veiled insincerity lurking beneath their genteel words. "I assure you, ladies, that both Bingley and I are exceedingly content and eagerly anticipate the radiant futures awaiting us with our respective brides."

Bingley, oblivious as ever, clapped Darcy on the back with a hearty chuckle. "Capital idea! We shall have a double wedding, Louisa - isn't it splendid?"

Louisa mustered a wan smile for her brother, already envisioning the inevitable awkward family gatherings looming on the horizon.

"How perfectly charming," Caroline managed to utter through clenched teeth, her words dripping with feigned delight.

As the sisters endeavored to maintain their composure, Bingley slapped Darcy's shoulder once more, his own joy untarnished. "Come, let us leave my sisters to their musings and return to our beloveds," he proposed, eyes alight with excitement.

At Longbourn, Elizabeth found herself attended by her diligent maid, who fussed over her mud-streaked gown and damp curls clinging to her flushed cheeks. Now enveloped in a simple yet elegant dress, Elizabeth eagerly anticipated the lively discussions sure to ensue in the wake of the day's exciting events.

Downstairs, Mrs. Bennet continued to regale her remaining daughters with animated plans for lavish weddings, sumptuous feasts, and fashionable new gowns. "Oh, my dear girls! Just imagine the envious whispers of all our neighbors when they see you two wedded to such affluent, dashing men!"

Kitty sighed dreamily at her mother's expressive words while Mary offered her sage thoughts on the subject. "As Proverbs 18:22 states, 'He who finds a wife finds a good thing and obtains favor from the Lord.' It seems our sisters have indeed been blessed."

Mr. Darcy and Mr. Bingley approached Longbourn, their horses' hooves creating a rhythmic symphony upon the gravel path leading up to the house. The familiar estate, basking in the golden glow of the afternoon sun, seemed to rejoice in the happiness radiating from the two approaching gentlemen.

Upon entering the house, the men were greeted with the warmth and laughter that filled the Bennet household. Elizabeth and Jane, upon detecting the arrival of their fiancés, hurried to the entrance hall to welcome them, their eyes shimmering with unbridled joy.

Bingley grinned broadly at Jane, his eyes sparkling. "We simply could not bear to be parted from you both for any longer," he declared, tenderly taking Jane's delicate hands in his own.

"And I found it quite unbearable to spend another moment apart from you, Elizabeth," added Mr. Darcy, his intense gaze locked on hers, conveying the profound depths of his affection.

Elizabeth's heart swelled at his tender profession. All remnants of past tensions dissolved in the warmth of his ardent devotion.

Stepping forward to claim her hands, Mr. Darcy lifted them to his lips. "My love, you have made me the happiest of men today. I pray I can spend every day proving myself worthy of your trust and esteem."

Elizabeth's eyes glistened. "As you have mine, Fitzwilliam," she smiled impishly, "though you nearly drowned in the attempt."

Mr. Darcy laughed. "A small price to pay for winning your hand, my darling."

Drawn together as if by unseen strings, their lips met in a sweet, lingering kiss, the world around them receding until nothing remained but the two of them, blissfully entwined in their own private Eden.

Their shared moment of intimacy concluded with quiet sighs as they reluctantly pulled away from each other, keenly aware of the presence of their family nearby.

"Well, we are most certainly delighted to see you again," Elizabeth replied, her heart swelling with happiness. "Now let us go inside and join my family for tea. I am certain my mother has prepared an extravagant spread in your honor."

Mrs. Bennet, eager to greet her future sons-in-law, bustled after her daughters, her excitement all but palpable. "Mr. Darcy, Mr. Bingley, how delightful to see you both. Do come in and join us for tea," she enthused, gesturing towards the drawing room where Kitty and Mary sat.

Mr. Bennet stood near the fireplace, observing the lively scene with a mixture of amusement and satisfaction. As he caught Mr. Darcy's eye, he extended his hand, exchanging the customary pleasantries before addressing him earnestly.

"I trust you will make my Lizzy happy, sir," he said, extending his hand to Mr. Darcy.

"I shall do everything in my power to ensure her happiness, Mr. Bennet," Mr. Darcy replied solemnly, clasping Mr. Bennet's hand firmly.

With an approving nod, Mr. Bennet relinquished his hold, allowing the couple some much-needed privacy.

Exchanging affectionate glances, Mr. Darcy and Elizabeth's eyes conveyed the unspoken depths of their feelings as they reveled in each other's company. Amidst the lively chatter and laughter that filled the room, they remained ensconced in their own blissful world, attuned solely to one another.

"I must admit," Elizabeth confessed with a conspiratorial smile, her voice barely more than a whisper, "that these recent events have been quite the dizzying dance. Yet knowing that we shall venture forth hand in hand fills me with a sense of comfort and happiness words cannot fully capture."

Mr. Darcy responded, his voice low and tender, the corners of his lips tinged with mischief, "Elizabeth, my dearest love, our journey thus far has indeed been peppered with unexpected twists and turns, but it is in navigating these challenges that we've discovered the depth of our connection. I eagerly anticipate embarking on this new chapter. Your love and support set my heart ablaze with joy beyond measure."

Their muffled laughter harmonized with the animated sounds of conversation from the family surrounding them. The couple shared an intimate glance, feeling as though they alone held the key to the language of their hearts. Jane and Bingley, seated nearby, caught their gaze and exchanged knowing smiles, basking in their shared happiness.

From his vantage point by the fireplace, Mr. Bennet observed the couples with keen interest, pride, and satisfaction bubbling within him as he witnessed the radiant happiness of his daughters. Clearing his throat to command the room's attention, he raised his glass, offering a toast laced with wit and warmth.

"To the union of two remarkable couples," he began, his voice resonant with both playfulness and sincerity, "may you embark on this next chapter enfolded in love, support, and a lifetime of felicity - and perhaps just a dash of intrigue!"

The room resonated with the melodious clinking of glasses and joyous exclamations of agreement as Elizabeth and Mr. Darcy continued to steal smoldering glances at one another. Their hearts brimmed with anticipation reassured that they were entering this new chapter of their lives hand in hand, a thrilling undercurrent of passion coursing between them.

~

MERYTON BUZZED with gossip about the upcoming nuptials in the days that followed. Neighbors whispered excitedly about the Bennet sisters, who had managed to secure not one, but two highly desirable matches. The ladies of the town, both young and old, sighed wistfully at the thought of the handsome and wealthy gentlemen who would soon be wed to local girls.

Whispers and knowing winks were exchanged among the villagers as they marveled at the lucky turn of events for the Bennet sisters. "To think," one astounded matron exclaimed, "that our dear Elizabeth has ensnared none other than Mr. Darcy himself! What a dazzling triumph for the Bennet family!"

Meanwhile, as the days leading up to the wedding neared, Elizabeth and Mr. Darcy found themselves stealing quiet moments together, delighting in each other's company amid the whirlwind of preparations. Their eyes would meet over morning tea or during stolen embraces in secluded garden nooks, feeling the magnetic pull of their burgeoning passion.

On the other hand, Caroline Bingley was utterly devastated by Mr. Darcy's engagement to Elizabeth. Her carefully concealed jealousy bubbled to the surface when she permitted herself a rare moment of vulnerability, harsh sobs echoing through her chambers as she mourned the loss of her most fervent aspiration.

As the momentous day approached, both Longbourn and Netherfield buzzed with activity as if possessed by spirited sprites eager to ensure an impeccable double wedding. Mrs. Bennet bustled about, issuing orders and muttering under her breath about lush floral arrangements, silk ribbons of the finest quality, and towering cakes adorned with intricate confections.

"I shall not have my daughters' special day marred by any mishaps," she declared, her cheeks rosy with determination, "Everything must be absolutely exquisite!"

Despite the heady mix of anticipation and anxiety that consumed so many involved in the upcoming celebration, Elizabeth and Mr. Darcy found solace in one another's arms during those fleeting moments of quietude. Their whispered words of love and devotion murmured beneath the silvery moonlight, served as a reminder that amidst the swirling chaos of life, they had found a sanctuary in each other.

As the sun ascended on the fateful morning when Elizabeth Bennet would become Mrs. Darcy and Jane Bennet would become Mrs. Bingley, the village of Meryton seemed to hold its breath, eagerly awaiting the enchantment and romance that was sure to unfold.

"Today is the day, Lizzy," Jane sighed, her voice lilting with happiness, "the commencement of our new lives."

Elizabeth squeezed her sister's hand affectionately. "Indeed, dear Jane, and what a splendid adventure awaits us both!"

As the sisters prepared for their momentous day, Mrs. Bennet orchestrated the household into a whirlwind, ensuring every detail was flawlessly executed. The melodious chatter of the servants harmonized with the bustle of activity below the stairs as they expertly transformed Longbourn into a veritable fairyland for the double nuptials.

Meanwhile, Mr. Darcy found himself pacing the opulent chambers at Netherfield, his long fingers absentmindedly ruffling his dark locks as he contemplated the magnitude of the day that lay before him.

Ever the embodiment of festive cheer, Bingley clapped his friend on the back, grinning like a schoolboy about to embark on a holiday. "Nervous, Darcy?" Bingley teased, his eyes alight with excitement. "I daresay you have nothing to fear. Elizabeth loves you dearly. We are both fortunate men to have won the hearts of such extraordinary women."

Mr. Darcy let out a soft chuckle, his countenance warming at the mention of Elizabeth's love. "Indeed, Bingley, we are truly blessed."

At Longbourn, the bride's chamber brimmed with effervescent anticipation as Elizabeth and Jane were artfully enveloped in sumptuous silks and delicate lace. Their younger sister, Kitty, lounged nearby, her eyes wide with wonder as she took in the scene before her.

"Oh, Lizzy, Jane," she breathed, "you both look absolutely resplendent. I can scarce believe this day has finally arrived!"

As the final golden hour of anticipation trickled away like sand through an hourglass, the inhabitants of Meryton congregated at the local church, a collective murmur of delight echoing through the air as they eagerly awaited their first glimpse of the radiant brides.

Elizabeth felt a shiver ripple through her as Mr. Darcy's smoldering gaze locked onto her own, his eyes ablaze with passion and promise. The weight of societal expectation seemed to dissipate at that moment, replaced by an electric current that hummed between them, igniting the air with longing.

And so, with hearts brimming with hope and love, Elizabeth Bennet and Fitzwilliam Darcy, as well as Jane Bennet and Charles Bingley, embarked on their new lives together, united in marriage beneath the watchful eyes of friends, family, and the bustling community that had borne witness to their entwined journey towards happiness.

THE END

Made in the USA
Middletown, DE
05 June 2023